Stephen Vincent
BENÉT

SHORT
STORIES

présenté par

Mᵐᵉ **BESSON**

Agrégée de l'Université.

British Library Cataloguing-in-Publication Data
A catalogue record for this book is available from the
British Library

Stephen Vincent Benét

Stephen Vincent Benét was born on 22nd July 1898 in Bethlehem, Pennsylvania, United States.

Benét was sent to the Hitchcock Military Academy at the age of ten and then continued his education at The Albany Academy in New York. He also attended Yale University where he received his M.A. in English.

Benét was an accomplished writer at an early age, having had his first book published at 17 and submitting his third volume of poetry in lieu of a thesis for his degree. During his time at Yale, he was an influential figure at the 'Yale Lit' literary magazine, and a fellow member of the Elizabethan Club. Benét was also a part-time contributor for the early Time Magazine.

Benét's involvement with the University literary scene led to a decade-long judgeship of the Yale Series of Younger Poets Competition. He is also responsible for publishing the first volumes of work by authors such as James Agee, Muriel Rukeyser, Jeremy Ingalls, and Margaret Walker. In 1931, he was elected as a fellow of the American Academy of Arts ad Sciences.

Benét's best known works are the book-length narrative poem *American Civil War, John Brown's Body* (1928), for which he won a Pulitzer Prize in 1929, and two short stories, *The Devil and Daniel Webster* (1936) and *By the Waters of Babylon* (1937). Benét won a second Pulitzer Prize posthumously for his unfinished poem *Western Star* in 1944.

Stephen Vincent Benét died of a heart attack in New York City, on 13th March, 1943, and is buried in Evergreen Cemetery, Stonington, Conneticut.

CONTENTS

ACKNOWLEDGMENTS

The editor and publisher express their gratitude to Messrs Farrar and Rinehart for kindly authorizing the publication of the following extracts. For the illustrations due acknowledgment in made to the U. S. Information Services.

INTRODUCTION

THOUGH *but little known in France, Stephen Vincent Benét was, before his recent death, one of the foremost figures in contemporary American literature.*

He was born in 1898 in Bethleem and belonged to a family of writers.

Benét passed most of his boyhood in Benicia (California). He went to school there, and later on in Georgia, and then to Yale University where he graduated. Afterwards he went to the Sorbonne and met his wife-to-be in Paris. Writing was henceforth his only profession. He had already, at seventeen, published six dramatic monologues in verse.

For a few years after his marriage, he depended for a living on his stories and novels, and these were lean years. Then luck came in the shape of a Guggenheim fellowship. He took his family to Paris, and there wrote his famous poem John Brown's Body *(1928). The talent for the ballad form, emotional patriotism, and knowledge of the period displayed in it, gained him the Pulitzer prize for poetry in 1929. His next success was a prose story,* The Devil and Daniel Webster, *a minor American classic which was turned into a grand opera. Benét himself later on wrote an operetta based on Washington Irving's* Legend of Sleepy Hollow.

He became a staff reviewer for the Saturday Review of Literature *and a member of the American Academy of Arts and Letters. He had left Paris for Rhode Island, and in the year 1930, he settled in New York. When the war came, he put aside his own work and devoted his energy and genius to the service of his country. Millions of Americans heard his great Radio Programs. Millions heard the* Prayer *for*

United Nations *read by President Roosevelt on Flag Day and written for the occasion by S. V. Benét. At the time of his tragic death in March 1943, he held a position probably never before achieved by an American writer. There have been unprecedented tributes to his memory, the affectionate recognition due to a great man.*

His achievement as a poet is generally admitted to be uneven. His novels are the least successful part of his work; but not so, his short stories, which are "ballads in prose" stamped with authenticity and a genuine folkloric flavour.

The two stories presented here are typical of S. V. Benét's talent as a story-teller and show what the author was interested in: America and the Americans. Nothing could be less metaphysical than his treatment of the eternal themes of life and death: the dreaded fool-killer is a petty official in the great administrative scheme of the universe; for heaven, like the earth, is a bureaucracy. His hero, Johnny Pye, moves us because he is so human.

Johnny, a middle-class boy of good abilities, attracts us by his earnestness, but also by his perfect ordinariness; his problems are our problems; if he is a fool, so are we all.

The second story, By the Waters of Babylon, *is inspired by the author's preoccupation with the destiny of his country. He wrote several poems on the subject of the America of the past. In the present story, we find another aspect of the picture. Centuries have gone past. Forests have taken the place of the dead cities and are inhabited by savages. One of them, brought up, like his brothers, in the belief that the builders were Gods, finds out that they were men like themselves who lived and died in a cataclysm.*

Homely and humorous, or fantastic, the two stories have a common link, the personality of the author, to whom might have been fitly applied his own definition of the destiny of Americans (in his poem The Western Star*):* " Americans are moving on ".

STEPHEN VINCENT BENÉT

SHORT STORIES

JOHNNY PYE AND THE FOOL-KILLER

I. HOW JOHNNY RAN AWAY
FROM THE FOOL-KILLER

You don't hear so much about the Fool-Killer these days, but when *Johnny *Pye was a boy there was a good deal of talk about him. Some said he was one kind of person, and some said another, but most people agreed that he came around fairly regular. Or, it seemed so to Johnny Pye. 5 But then, Johnny was an *adopted child, which is, maybe, why he took it so hard.

The miller and his wife had offered to raise him, after his own folks died, and that was a good deed on their part. But, as soon as he lost his baby teeth and started acting the 10 way most boys act, they started to come down on him like thunder, which wasn't so good. They were good people, according to their lights, but their lights were terrible strict ones, and they believed that the harder you were on a *youngster, the better and brighter he got. Well, that may 15 work with some children, but it didn't with Johnny Pye.

He was sharp enough and willing enough—as sharp and willing as most boys in *Martinsville. But, somehow or other, he never seemed to be able to do the right things or say the right words—at least when he was home. Treat a 20 boy like a fool and he'll act like a fool, I say, but there's some folks need *convincing. The miller and his wife

2. ˈdʒɔnɪ; paɪ. — 6. əˈdɔptɪd. — 15. ˈjʌŋstə. -- 18. ˈmɑːtɪnzvil. — 22. kənˈvɪnsɪŋ.

thought the way to smarten Johnny was to treat him like a
fool, and finally they got so he pretty much believed it him-
25 self.

And that was hard on him, for he had a boy's imagina-
tion, and maybe a little more than most. He could stand
the beatings and he did. But what he couldn't stand was
the way things went at the mill. I don't suppose the miller
30 intended to do it. But, as long as Johnny Pye could remember, whenever he heard of the death of somebody he didn't
like, he'd say : " Well, the Fool-Killer's come for so-and-
so, " and sort of smack his lips. It was, as you might say, a
family joke, but the miller was a big man with a big red face,
35 and it made a strong impression on Johnny Pye. Till,
finally, he got a picture of the Fool-Killer, himself. He was
a big man, too, in a checked shirt and *corduroy trousers,
and he went walking the ways of the world, with a *hickory
club that had a lump of lead in the end of it. I don't know
40 how Johnny Pye got that picture so clear, but, to him, it was
just as plain as the face of any human being in Martinsville.
And, now and then, just to test it, he'd ask a grown-up
person, kind of timidly, if that was the way the Fool-Killer
looked. And, of course, they'd generally laugh and tell
45 him it was. Then Johnny would wake up at night, in his
room over the mill, and listen for the Fool-Killer's step on
the road and wonder when he was coming. But he was
brave enough not to tell anybody that.

Finally, though, things got a little more than he could
50 bear. He'd done some boy's trick or other—let the stones
grind a little fine, maybe, when the miller wanted the meal
ground coarse—just carelessness, you know. But he'd gotten two whippings for it, one from the miller and one from
his wife, and at the end of it, the miller had said : " Well,
55 Johnny Pye, the Fool-Killer ought to be along for you most
any day now. For I never did see a boy that was such a
fool. " Johnny looked to the miller's wife to see if she
believed it, too, but she just shook her head and looked

37. 'kɔ:djurɔi. — 38. 'hɪkərɪ.

*serious. So he went to bed that night, but he couldn't sleep, for every time a *bough *rustled or the mill wheel 60 creaked, it seemed to him it must be the Fool-Killer. And, early next morning, before anybody was up, he packed such duds as he had in a *bandanna *handkerchief and ran away.

He didn't really expect to get away from the Fool-Killer very long—as far as he knew, the Fool-Killer got you wher- 65 ever you went. But he thought he'd give him a run for his money, at least. And when he got on the road, it was a bright spring morning, and the first peace and quiet he'd had in some time. So his spirits rose, and he chunked a stone at a bullfrog as he went along, just to show he was 70 Johnny Pye and still doing business.

He hadn't gone more than three or four miles out of Martinsville, when he heard a buggy coming up the road behind him. He knew the Fool-Killer didn't need a buggy to catch you, so he wasn't afraid of it, but he stepped 75 to the side of the road to let it pass. But it stopped, instead, and a black-whiskered man with a stove-pipe hat looked out of it.

" Hello, bub, " he said. " Is this the road for East Liberty? " 80

" My name's John Pye and I'm eleven years old, " said Johnny, *polite but firm, " and you take the next left fork for East Liberty. They say it's a pretty town—I've never been there myself. " And he sighed a little, because he thought he'd like to see the world before the Fool-Killer 85 caught up with him.

" H'm, " said the man. " Stranger here, too, eh? And what brings a smart boy like you on the road so early in the morning? "

" Oh, " said Johnny Pye, quite *honestly, " I'm running 90 away from the Fool-Killer. For the miller says I'm a fool and his wife says I'm a fool and almost everybody in Mar- tinsville says I'm a fool except little *Susie *Marsh. And

---

59. 'siəriəs. — 60. bau; rʌsld. — 63. bæn'dænə; 'hæŋkətʃif. — 82. pə'lait. — 90. 'ɔnistli. — 93. 'suːzɪ; mɑːʃ.

the miller says the Fool-Killer's after me—so I thought I'd
95 run away before he came."

The black-whiskered man sat in his buggy and wheezed
for a while. When he got his breath back, " Well, jump
in, bub, " he said. " The miller may say you're a fool, but
I think you're a right smart boy to be running away from
100 the Fool-Killer all by yourself. And I don't hold with
small-town *prejudices and I need a right smart boy, so
I'll give you a lift on the road. "

" But, will I be safe from the Fool-Killer, if I'm with
you? " said Johnny. " For, *otherwise, it don't *signify. "
105 " Safe? " said the black-whiskered man, and wheezed
again. " Oh, you'll be safe as houses. You see, I'm a herb
doctor—and some folks think, a little in the Fool-Killer's
line of business, myself. And I'll teach you a trade worth
two of milling. So jump in, bub. "
110 " Sounds all right the way you say it, " said Johnny,
" but my name's Johnny Pye, " and he jumped into the
buggy. And they went rattling along toward East Liberty
with the herb doctor talking and cutting jokes till Johnny
thought he'd never met a pleasanter man. About half a
115 mile from East Liberty, the doctor stopped at a spring.

" What are we stopping here for? " said Johnny Pye.

" Wait and see, " said the doctor, and gave him a wink.
Then he got a *haircloth trunk full of empty bottles out of
the back of the buggy and made Johnny fill them with
120 spring water and *label them. Then he added a pinch of
pink powder to each bottle and shook them up and corked
them and stowed them away.

" What's that? " said Johnny, very interested.

" That's Old Doctor *Waldo's *Unparalleled *Universal
125 *Remedy, " said the doctor, reading from the label. " Made
from the *purest snake oil and *secret Indian herbs, it cures

---

101. 'predʒudisɪz. — 104. 'ʌðəwaɪz; 'sɪgnifaɪ. — 118. 'hɛəklɔːθ.
— 120. leɪbl. — 124. 'wɔːldou; ʌn'pærələld; ˌjuːni'vəːsəl. — 125.
remidi. — 126. 'pjuərist; siːkrit.

*rheumatism, blind staggers, *headache, *malaria, five kinds
of fits, and spots in front of the eyes. It will also *remove
oil or grease stains, clean knives and silver, polish brass, and
is strongly recommended as a general tonic and blood puri-   130
fier. Small size, one dollar—family bottle, two dollars and
a half. "

" But I don't see any snake oil in it, " said Johnny,
puzzled, " or any secret Indian herbs. "

" That's because you're not a fool, " said the doctor,   135
with another wink. " The Fool-Killer wouldn't, either.
But most folks will. "

And, that very same night, Johnny saw. For the doctor
made his pitch in East Liberty and he did it handsome. He
took a couple of flaring oil torches and stuck them on the   140
sides of the buggy; he put on a * diamond stickpin and did
card tricks and told funny stories till he had the crowd
goggle-eyed. As for Johnny, he let him play on the *tam-
bourine. Then he started talking about Doctor Waldo's
Universal Remedy, and, with Johnny to help him, the   145
bottles went like hot cakes. Johnny helped the doctor
count the money afterward, and it was a pile.

" Well, " said Johnny, " I never saw money made easier.
You've got a fine trade, doctor. "

" It's cleverness does it, " said the doctor, and slapped   150
him on the back. " Now a fool's *content to stay in one
place and do one thing, but the Fool-Killer never caught up
with a good pitchman yet. "

" Well, it's certainly lucky I met up with you, " said
Johnny, " and, if it's cleverness does it, I'll learn the trade   155
or bust. "

So he stayed with the doctor quite a while—in fact, till
he could make up the remedy and do the card tricks almost
as good as the doctor himself. And Johnny admired the
doctor and the doctor liked Johnny, for Johnny was a bid-   160
dable boy. But one night they came into a town where

---

127. 'ruːmətizm; 'hedeik; məˈlɛərɪə. — 128. rɪˈmuːv. — 141. 'daiə-
mənd. — 143. ˌtæmbəˈriːn. — 151. kənˈtent.

things didn't go as they usually did. The crowd gathered as usual, and the doctor did his tricks. But, all the time, Johnny could see a sharp-faced little fellow going through
165 the crowd and whispering to one man and another. Till, at last, right in the middle of the doctor's *spiel, the sharp-faced fellow gave a shout of " That's him all right ! I'd know them whiskers anywhere ! " and, with that, the crowd growled once and began to tear slats out of the
170 nearest fence. Well, the next thing Johnny knew, he and the doctor were being ridden out of town on a rail, with the doctor's long coattails flying at every jounce.

They didn't hurt Johnny *particular—him only being a boy. But they warned 'em both never to show their
175 faces in that town again, and then they heaved the doctor into a *thistle patch and went their ways.

" *Owoo ! " said the doctor, " *ouch ! " as Johnny was helping him out of the thistle patch. " Go easy with those thistles ! And why didn't you give me the office, you
180 blame little fool? "

" Office? " said Johnny. " What office? "

" When that sharp-nosed man started snooping around, " said the doctor. " I thought that *infernal main street looked *familiar—I was through there two years ago, sel-
185 ling solid gold watches for a dollar apiece. "

" But the works to a solid gold watch would be worth more than that, " said Johnny.

" There weren't any works, " said the doctor, with a groan, " but there was a nice little beetle inside each case
190 and it made the prettiest tick you ever heard. "

" Well, that certainly was a clever idea ", said Johnny. " I'd never have thought of that. "

" Clever? " said the doctor. " Ouch—it was *ruina-tion ! But who'd have thought the fools would bear a
195 grudge for two years? And now we've lost the horse and buggy, too—not to speak of the bottles and the money.

166. ʃpiːl. — 173. pəˈtikjulə. — 176. θisl. — 177. ˈouwou;autʃ. — 183. inˈfəːnəl. — 184. fəˈmiljə. — 193. ruiˈneiʃən.

Well, there's lots more tricks to be played and we'll start again. "

But, though he liked the doctor, Johnny began to feel *dubious. For it occurred to him that, if all the doctor's 200 cleverness got him was being ridden out of town on a rail, he couldn't be so far away from the Fool-Killer as he thought. And, sure enough, as he was going to sleep that night, he seemed to hear the Fool-Killer's footsteps coming after him—step, step, step. He pulled his jacket up over 205 his ears, but he couldn't shut it out. So, when the doctor had got in the way of starting business over again, he and Johnny parted *company. The doctor didn't bear any grudge; he shook hands with Johnny and told him to remember that cleverness was *power. And Johnny 210 went on with his running away.· He got to a town, and there was a store with a sign in the window, BOY WANTED, so he went in.

There, sure enough, was the merchant, sitting at his desk, and a fine, important man he looked, in his black broad- 215 cloth *suit. Johnny tried to tell him about the Fool-Killer, but the merchant wasn't *interested in that. He just looked Johnny over and saw that he looked biddable and strong for his age. " But, remember, no fooling around, boy ! " said the merchant sternly, after he'd hired 220 him.

" No fooling around? " said Johnny, with the light of hope in his eyes.

" No, " said the merchant, meaningly. " We've no room for fools in this business, I can tell you! You work 225 hard, and you'll rise. But, if you've got any foolish notions, just knock them on the head and forget them. "

Well, Johnny was glad enough to *promise that, and he stayed with the merchant a year and a half. He swept out the store, and he put the shutters up and took them down; 230 he ran *errands and *wrapped up *packages and learned to

---

200. 'djuːbiəs. — 208. 'kʌmpəni. — 210. pauə. — 216. sjuːt. —
217. 'intristid. — 228. 'prɔmis. — 231. 'erəndz; ræpt; pækidʒiz.

keep busy twelve hours a day. And, being a biddable boy and an honest one, he rose, just like the merchant had said. The merchant raised his wages and let him begin to wait
235 on customers and learn accounts. And then, one night, Johnny woke up in the middle of the night. And it seemed to him he heard, far away but getting nearer, the steps of the Fool-Killer after him—tramping, tramping.

He went to the merchant next day and said: " Sir, I'm
240 sorry to tell you this, but I'll have to be moving on. "

" Well, I'm sorry to hear that, Johnny, " said the merchant, " for you've been a good boy. And, if it's a question of salary—— "

" It isn't that, " said Johnny, " but tell me one thing, sir,
245 if you don't mind my asking. Supposing I did stay with you—where would I end? "

The merchant smiled. " That's a hard question to answer, " he said, " and I'm not much given to compliments. But I started, myself, as a boy, sweeping out the
250 store. And you're a bright youngster with lots of *go-ahead. I don't see why, if you stuck to it, you shouldn't make the same kind of *success that I have. "

" And what's that? " said Johnny.

The merchant began to look *irritated, but he kept his
255 smile.

" Well, " he said, " I'm not a boastful man, but I'll tell you this. Ten years ago I was the richest man in town. Five years ago, I was the richest man in the county. And five years from now—well, I aim to be the richest man in
260 the state. "

His eyes kind of glittered as he said it, but Johnny was looking at his face. It was *sallow-skinned and * pouchy, with the jaw as hard as a rock. And it came upon Johnny that moment that, though he'd known the merchant a year
265 and a half, he'd never really seen him enjoy himself except when he was driving a *bargain.

---

250. ˌgouə'hed. — 252. sək'ses. — 254. 'ırıteitıd. — 262. 'sælou-skınd; 'pautʃı. — 266. 'bɑːgın.

A MODERN " MERCHANT " IN HIS STORE.

" Sorry, sir ", he said, " but, if it's like that, I'll certainly have to go. Because, you see, I'm running away from the Fool-Killer, and, if I stayed here and got to be like you,
270 he'd certainly catch up with me in no—— "

" Why, you *impertinent young cub ! " roared the merchant, with his face gone red all of a sudden. " Get your money from the *cashier ! " and Johnny was on the road again before you could say " Jack *Robinson. " But, this
275 time, he was used to it, and walked off whistling.

Well, after that, he hired out to quite a few different people, but I won't go into all of his *adventures. He worked for an inventor for a while, and they split up because Johnny happened to ask him what would be the good of
280 his *patent, self-winding, *perpetual-motion *machine, once he did get it invented. And, while the inventor talked big about improving the human race and the beauties of *science, it was plain he didn't know. So that night, Johnny heard the steps of the Fool-Killer, far off but coming closer,
285 and, next morning, he went away. Then he stayed with a minister for a while, and he certainly hated to leave him, for the minister was a good man. But they got talking one evening and, as it chanced, Johnny asked him what happened to people who didn't believe in his particular religion.
290 Well, the minister was broad-minded, but there's only one answer to that. He admitted they might be good folks—he even admitted they mightn't exactly go to hell—but he couldn't let them into heaven, no, not the best and the wisest of them, for there were the *specifications laid down
295 by creed and church, and, if you didn't fulfill them, you didn't.

So Johnny had to leave him, and, after that, he went with an old drunken fiddler for a while. He wasn't a good man, I guess, but he could play till the tears ran down your
300 cheeks. And, when he was playing his best, it seemed to Johnny that the Fool-Killer was very far away. For, in spite

271. im'pɔːtinənt. — 273 kæ'ʃiə. — 274. 'rɔbinsən. — 277. əd-'ventʃəz. — 280. 'peitənt; pə'petjuəl; mə'ʃiːn. — 283. saiəns. — 294. ˌspesifi'kəiʃənz.

of his faults and his weaknesses, while he played, there was
might in the man.   But he died drunk in a ditch, one night,
with Johnny to hold his head, and, while he left Johnny
his fiddle, it didn't do Johnny much good.   For, while 305
Johnny could play a tune, he couldn't play like the fiddler
—it wasn't in his fingers.

Then it *chanced that Johnny took up with a company of
*soldiers.   He was still too young to *enlist, but they made
a kind of pet of him, and everything went swimmingly for 310
a while.   For the captain was the bravest man Johnny had
ever seen, and he had an answer for everything, out of
regulations and the Articles of War.   But then they went
West to fight Indians and the same old trouble cropped up
again.   For, one night the captain said to him : " Johnny, 315
we're going to fight the *enemy tomorrow, but you'll stay
in camp. "

" Oh, I don't want to do that, " said Johnny; " I want to
be in on the fighting. "

" It's an order, " said the captain, grimly.   Then he 320
gave Johnny certain instructions and a letter to take to his
wife.

" For the *colonel's a copper-plated fool, " he said, " and
we're walking straight into an *ambush. "

" Why don't you tell him that? " said Johnny.   325
" I have, " said the captain, " but he's the colonel. "

" Colonel or no colonel, " said Johnny, " if he's a fool,
somebody ought to stop him. "

" You can't do that, in an army, " said the captain.
" Orders are orders. "   But it turned out the captain was 330
wrong about it, for, next day, before they could get moving,
the Indians attacked, and got badly licked.   When it was
all over, " Well, it was a good fight, " said the captain,
*professionally.   " All the same, if they'd waited and laid
an ambush, they'd have had our hair.   But, as it was, they 335
didn't stand a chance. "

---

308. tʃɑːnst. — 309. 'souldʒəz; in'list. — 316. 'enimi. — 323.
kəːnəl. — 324. 'æmbuʃ. — 334. prə'feʃənəli.

"But why didn't they lay an ambush? " said Johnny.
"Well, " said the captain, " I guess they had their orders
too. And now, how would you like to be a soldier? "

340 "Well, it's a nice outdoors life, but I'd like to think it
over," said Johnny. For he knew the captain was brave
and he knew the Indians had been brave—you couldn't
find two braver sets of people. But, all the same when he
thought the whole thing over, he seemed to hear steps in the
345 sky. So he soldiered to the end of the *campaign and then
he left the Army, though the captain told him he was
making a mistake.

345. kæm'pein.

NOTES

4. agreed : were of the same opinion. — **5.** fairly regular : fairly regularly (the author often uses the adjective instead of the adverb). — **7.** so hard : so seriously. — **9.** folks : parents. — **11.** to come down on : to punish. — **13.** terrible : see note on l.5. — **16.** work : produce a result. — **18.** willing : cheerfully ready to do things; somehow or other : for various, undetermined reasons. — **20.** (at) home. — **23.** to smarten : to make more intelligent. — **24.** they got so : they produced the result that; pretty much : almost. — **27.** stand : endure. — **32.** he *would* say; *has* come; so-and-so : *Untel*. — **33.** sort of : almost, if not exactly; smack his lips : make with his lips a slight explosive noise in eager anticipation of pleasure. — **37.** checked : printed with a cross-lined pattern; corduroy: *velours côtelé*. — **38.** hickory : *noyer blanc*. — **42.** test : control. — **50.** trick : foolish act; the (grinding-) stones of the mill : *les meules*. — **51.** meal : flour. — **52.** coarse : large in grain; gotten : (familiar for) got. — **55.** to be (coming) along for you (al)most. — **63.** duds : (slang for) clothes; bandanna : richly coloured yellow or white-spotted silk. — **66.** give him a run for his money : *lui faire gagner son argent*. — **69.** spirits : energy; chunked : threw. — **70.** bullfrog : *grosse grenouille*. — **73.** buggy : light horse-drawn vehicle. — **77.** stove-pipe hat : « *tuyau de poêle* ». — **79.** bub : (familiar for) friend. — **96.** wheezed : breathed with audible friction. — **100.** hold with : approve of. — **102.** give you a lift : take you into my vehicle for part of the road. — **104.** otherwise : if it is not so; it don't (doesn't) signify : it is not worth while. — **108.** line of business : *branche;* worth two of : worth twice as much as. — **112.** rattling : driving briskly with a succession of short, sharp sounds. — **117.** a wink : the act of closing one eye. — **118.** haircloth : *étoffe de crin*. — **122.** stowed away : packed them out of sight. — **127.** staggers : *vertigo* (a disease of sheep). — **128.** fits : *attaques*. — **139.** made his pitch : erected his tent; handsome(ly). — **140.** flaring : blazing with a bright unsteady flame. — **143.** goggle-eyed : with eyes protuberant and rolling with astonishment. — **146.** went like hot cakes : were sold rapidly. — **153.** pitchman : itinerant vendor. — **154.** I met up with you : (vulgar for) I met you. — **155.** if it's cleverness (that) does it. — **156.** bust : (vulgar for) die. — **159.** good : well. — **160.** biddable : who did what he was bidden (ordered) to do. — **166.** right : just; spiel : a German word, meaning play. — **167-168.** (vulgar for) That is really he ! I should know (recognize) those whiskers anywhere ! — **169.** slats : thin, narrow pieces of wood. — **171.** ridden out of town on a rail : obliged to leave the town riding on a rail (bar). — **172.** jounce : jolt, shake. — **174.** (th)em. — **175.** heaved : threw. — **176.** thistle : *chardon*. — **179.** give the office : (slang for) make a signal — **182.** snoop : move or look furtively. — **186.** the works : *le mouvement*. — **189.** beetle : *scarabée*. — **194.** bear a grudge : persist in anger. — **197.** there are *many other* tricks. — **200.** dubious : full of doubts. — **203.** sure enough : *cela ne manqua pas*. — **206.** shut it out : prevent the noise of the Fool-Killer's steps from being heard. — **212.** store : large shop. — **215.** broadcloth : *drap fin*. — **218.** looked... over : examined. — **219.** fooling around : amusing oneself stupidly. — **220.** hired : taken in his service. — **226.** rise : reach a higher position. — **231.** ran errands : *fit des commissions*. — **233.** like : as. — **234.** wait on : serve. — **238.** tramping : walking heavily. — **240.** I'll have : I shall be obliged. — **245.** if you don't mind : if you have no objection to. — **248.** given to compliments : accustomed to pay com-

pliments. — **250.** go-ahead : energy — **251.** stuck : applied yourself persistently. — **252.** that : as. — **261.** kind of : sort of (see note on l. 33). — **262.** sallow : pale and yellowish; pouchy : with the flesh forming pouches, especially under the eyes. — **266.** driving a bargain : coming to the conclusion of a commercial transaction. — **270.** in no- : (Johnny is going to add : time) very rapidly. — **271.** cub : the young of a bear (figuratively, an unpolished youth). — **272.** gone : become. — **274.** before you could say " Jack Robinson " : *en un tournemain*. — **276.** hired out to : entered the service of. — **278.** split up : separated. — **280.** patent : *brevetée;* once : after. — **281.** talked big : spoke with grandiloquence. — **286.** minister : clergyman; hated : deeply regretted. — **288.** chanced : happened. — **293.** let them into : let them enter. — **295.** creed : text summing up religious doctrine or belief; you didn't : nothing could be done about it. — **298.** fiddler : fiddle-(or violin-) player. — **303.** might : power. — **307.** it : the artistic power. — **308.** took up with : joined. — **310.** pet : favourite animal; swimmingly : happily and smoothly. — **314.** cropped up : presented itself. — **320.** grimly : severely. — **323.** copper-plated : elegant and perfect, like copper-plated writing *(calligraphie).* — **330.** it turned out : it became apparent. — **332.** licked : (slang for) beaten. — **334.** professionally : giving his opinion as a professional. — **335.** they'd have had our hair : they would have taken us prisoners and been able to scalp us. — **338.** guess : suppose. — **340.** think it over : reflect about it. — **345.** soldiered : led a military life.

THÈME D'IMITATION

Un commerce prospère.

Le docteur que rencontra Johnny avait un commerce mal-
honnête, mais prospère. Chaque fois qu'il arrivait dans une
nouvelle ville, de bonne heure le soir, il était assez adroit pour
attirer l'attention des gens. Il avait seulement besoin d'eau et de
quelques bouteilles avant de commencer sa vente miraculeuse.
Plus il parlait longuement, plus les gens lui donnaient d'argent.
Son succès dura un bon moment, mais tout à coup il eut de
graves ennuis. En un tournemain il perdit ce qu'il avait gagné.
Qui aurait cru que les choses se gâteraient si vite ?

VERSION AVEC QUESTIONS

An English miller's wife.

Mrs. Tulliver was what is called a good-tempered person —
never cried, when she was a baby, on any slighter ground than
hunger and pins; and from the cradle upwards had been healthy,
fair, plump and dull-witted; in short, the flower of her family
for beauty and amiability. But milk and mildness are not the
best things for keeping, and when they turn only a little sour,
they may disagree with young stomachs seriously. I have
often wondered whether those early Madonnas of Raphael,
with the blond faces and somewhat stupid expressions, kept
their placidity undisturbed when their strong-limbed, strong-
willed boys got a little too old to do without clothing. I think
they must have been given to feeble remonstrance, getting more
and more peevish as it became more and more ineffectual.
George ELIOT, *The Mill on the Floss.*

QUESTIONS : 1. *Was Johnny's adopted mother like Mrs. Tulliver?* — 2. *What details in this text show that Mrs. Tulliver
was not particularly clever?* — 3. *Describe a French miller's wife,
and try to make her different from Johnny's adopted mother, and
from Mrs. Tulliver.*

QUESTIONNAIRE

Do you believe in the real existence of the Fool-Killer? — Did Johnny Pye believe in it? — What do you think of his adopted parents' system of education? — Was Johnny an exceptional boy, for good or for bad? — How did Johnny picture to himself the physical appearance of the Fool-Killer? — Why did Johnny run away from the mill? — Where was the Doctor going when he saw Johnny for the first time? — What was the Doctor's trade? — What was his Universal Remedy good for? According to him? — And in fact? — How did the Doctor conduct his business? — How did Johnny help the Doctor? — What put an end to their association? — How would you like to be thrown into a thistle patch? — Why were the people angry at the Doctor? — What was Johnny's next profession? — Was he successful in it? — Why did he leave the merchant? — What did the merchant think of himself? — What did Johnny think of him? — What was Johnny's inventor inventing? — Why was the Fool-Killer near that inventor? — What happened to the fiddler? — What use was the fiddle to Johnny? — What did Johnny's captain think of his colonel? — Was he right? — When did Johnny leave the army? — What do you think of Johnny's career in those early years?

INTONATION

(Neutre, descendante, affirmation simple.)

9. and ⌐that was a ⌐good ⌐deed on their \ part ‖

(Neutre, descendante, question comportant un mot interrogatif.)

116. ⌐What are we \ stopping here for? ‖

(Neutre, ascendante; sous-entendu ironique.)

135. ⌐that's be-cause you're ₋not a ╱ fool ↑

(Neutre, descendante, ordre impératif.)

272. ⌐Get your ⌐money from the ca \ shier ‖

II. LOVE MAKES JOHNNY
FAIR GAME FOR THE FOOL-KILLER

By now, of course, he wasn't a boy any longer; he was getting to be a young man with a young man's thoughts and feelings. And, half the time, *nowadays, he'd *forget about the Fool-Killer except as a dream he'd had when he was a
5 boy. He could even laugh at it now and then, and think what a fool he'd been to believe there was such a man.

But, all the same, the *desire in him wasn't *satisfied, and something kept driving him on. He'd have called it *ambitiousness, now, but it came to the same thing. And with
10 every new trade he tried, sooner or later would come the dream—the dream of the big man in the checked shirt and *corduroy pants, walking the ways of the world with his hickory stick in one hand. It made him angry to have that dream, now, but it had a singular *power over him. Till,
15 *finally, when he was turned twenty or so, he got scared.

" Fool-Killer, or no Fool-Killer, " he said to himself, " I've got to *ravel this matter out. For there must be some one thing a man could tie to, and be sure he wasn't a fool. I've tried cleverness and money and half a *dozen other
20 things, and they don't seem to be the *answer. So now I'll try book learning and see what comes of that. "

So he read all the books he could find, and whenever he'd seem to hear the steps of the Fool-Killer coming for the *authors—and that was frequent—he'd try and shut his
25 ears. But some books said one thing was best and some another, and he couldn't rightly *decide.

" Well, " he said to himself, when he'd read and read till

3. 'nauədeiz; fə'get. — 7. di'zəiə; 'sætisfaid. — 8. æm'biʃəsnis. — 12. 'kɔːdjurɔi. — 14. pauə. — 15. 'fainəlı. — 17. 'rævl. — 19. 'dʌzn. — 20. 'ɑːnsə. — 24. 'ɔːθəz. — 26. di'said.

his head felt as stuffed with book learning as a *sausage with meat, " it's interesting, but it isn't *exactly *contemporaneous. So I think I'll go down to *Washington and ask the wise men there. For it must take a lot of wisdom to run a country like the United States, and if there's people who can answer my *questions, it's there they ought to be found. "

So he packed his bag and off to Washington he went. He was modest, for a youngster, and he didn't *intend to try and see the President right away. He thought probably a *congressman was about his size. So he saw a congressman, and the congressman told him the thing to be was an upstanding young American and vote the *Republican ticket—which sounded all right to Johnny Pye, but not exactly what he was after.

Then he went to a *senator, and the senator told him to be an upstanding young American and vote the *Democratic ticket—which sounded all right, too, but not what he was after, *either. And, somehow, though both men had been *impressive and *affable, right in the middle of their speeches he'd seemed to hear steps—you know.

But a man has to eat, whatever else he does, and Johnny found he'd better buckle down and get himself a job. It happened to be with the first congressman he struck, for that one came from Martinsville, which is why Johnny went to him in the first place. And, in a little while, he forgot his search *entirely and the Fool-Killer, too, for the congressman's niece came East to visit him, and she was the Susie Marsh that Johnny had sat next in school. She'd been *pretty then, but she was prettier now, and as soon as Johnny Pye saw her, his heart gave a jump and a thump.

" And don't think we don't remember you in Martinsville, Johnny Pye," she said, when her uncle had *explained

28. 'sɔsɪdʒ. — 29. ɪg'zæktli; kən‚tempə'reinjəs. — 30. 'wɔʃɪŋtən. 33. 'kwestʃənz. — 35. ɪn'tend. — 38. 'kɔŋgresmən. — 40. rɪ'pʌblɪkn. — 43. 'senətə. — 44. ‚demə'krætɪk. — 46. 'aɪðə. — 47. ɪm'presiv; 'æfəbl. — 54. ɪn'taiəlɪ. — 57. 'prɪtɪ. — 60. ɪks'pleɪnd.

who his new *clerk was. " Why, the whole town'll be
*excited when I write home. We've heard all about your
killing Indians and inventing perpetual motion and travel-
ling around the country with a famous doctor and making
65 a *fortune in dry goods and—oh, it's a *wonderful story ! ''
    " Well," said Johnny, and *coughed, " some of that's
just a little bit *exaggerated. But it's nice of you to be
interested. So they don't think I'm a fool any more, in
Martinsville ? ''
70   " I never thought you were a fool, " said Susie with a
little smile, and Johnny felt his heart give another bump.
    " And I always knew you were pretty, but never how
pretty till now ," said Johnny, and coughed again. " But,
speaking of old times, how's the miller and his wife ? For
75 I did leave them right sudden, and while there were *faults
on both sides, I must have been a *trial to them too. ''
    " They've gone the way of all flesh, " said Susie Marsh,
" and there's a new miller now. But he isn't very well-
liked, to tell the truth, and he's letting the mill run down. ''
80   " That's a pity, " said Johnny, " for it was a likely mill. ''
Then he began to ask her more questions and she began to
remember things too. Well, you know how the time can go
when two youngsters get talking like that.
    Johnny Pye never worked so hard in his life as he did
85 that winter. And it wasn't the Fool-Killer he thought
about—it was Susie Marsh. First he thought she loved him
and then he was sure she didn't, and then he was betwixt
and between, and all *perplexed and *confused. But,
*finally, it turned out all right and he had her *promise,
90 and Johnny Pye knew he was the *happiest man in the
world. And that night, he waked up in the night and
heard the Fool-Killer coming after him—step, step, step.
    He didn't sleep much after that, and he came down to

---

61. klɑːk. — 62. ikˈsaitid. — 65. ˈfɔːtʃən; ˈwʌndəfl.
— 66. kɔːft. — 67. igˈzæzʒəreitid. — 75. fɔːlts. — 76. traiəl. — 88. pəˈplekst;
kənˈfjuːzd. — 89. ˈfainəli; ˈprɔmis. — 90. ˈhæpust.

IN CONGRESS.

*breakfast *hollow-eyed. But his uncle-to-be didn't notice
95 that—he was rubbing his hands and smiling.

" Put on your best necktie, Johnny ! " he said, very cheer-
ful, " for I've got an *appointment with the President today,
and, just to show I *approve of my *niece's fiancé, I'm taking
you along. "

100   " The President ! " said Johnny, all *dumfounded.

" Yes, " said Congressman Marsh, " you see, there's a
little bill—well, we needn't go into that. But slick down
your back hair, Johnny—we'll make Martinsville proud of
us this day ! "

105   Then a weight seemed to go from Johnny's shoulders and
a load from his heart. He wrung Mr. Marsh's hand.

" Thank you, Uncle *Eben ! " he said. " I can't thank
you enough. " For, at last, he knew he was going to look
upon a man that was bound to be safe from the Fool-Killer
110 —and it seemed to him if he could just once do that, all his
*troubles and searchings would be ended.

Well, it doesn't signify which President it was—you can
take it from me that he was President and a fine-looking
man. He'd just been *elected, too, so he was lively as a
115 trout, and the saddle *galls he'd get from Congress hadn't
even begun to show. Anyhow, there he was, and Johnny
*feasted his eyes on him. For if there was anybody in the
country the Fool-Killer couldn't *bother, it must be a man
like this.

120   The President and the congressman talked *politics for a
while, and then it was Johnny's turn.

" Well, young man, " said the President, affably, " and
what can I do for you—for you look to me like a fine,
upstanding young American. "

125   The congressman cut in quick before Johnny could open
his mouth. " Just a word of *advice, Mr. President, " he
said. " Just a word in season. For my young friend's led

---

94. 'brekfəst; 'hɔlou ‚aid. — 97. ə'pɔintmənt. — 98. ə'pru:v;
'ni:sɪz. — 100. 'dʌmfaundid. — 107. 'i:bn. — 111. 'trʌblz. —
114. i'lektid. — 115. gɔ:lz. — 117. 'fi:stid. — 118. 'bɔðə. — 120.
'pɔlitiks. — 126. əd'vais.

an *adventurous life, but now he's going to marry my niece and settle down. And what he needs most of all is a word of ripe wisdom from you. "   130

" Well, " said the President, looking at Johnny rather keenly, " if that's all he needs, a short horse is soon *curried. I wish most of my callers wanted as little. "

But, all the same, he drew Johnny out, as such men can, and before Johnny knew it, he was telling his life story.   135

" Well, " said the President, at the end, " you certainly have been a rolling stone, young man. But there's nothing wrong in that. And, for one of your *varied *experience there's one obvious *career. Politics ! " he said, and slapped his fist in his hand.   140

" Well, " said Johnny, scratching his head, " of course, since I've been in Washington, I've thought of that. But I don't know that I'm rightly fitted. "

" You can write a speech, " said Congressman Marsh, quite thoughtful, " for you've helped me with mine. You're   145 a likable fellow too. And you were born poor and worked up—and you've even got a *war-record—why, hell ! *Excuse me, Mr. President !—he's worth five hundred votes just as he stands ! "

" I—I'm more than *honored by you two gentlemen, "   150 said Johnny, *abashed and flattered, " but *supposing I did go into politics—where would I end up? "

The President looked sort of *modest.

" The *Presidency of the United States, " said he, " is within the *legitimate *ambition of every American citizen.   155 *Provided he can get elected, of course. "

" Oh, " said Johnny, feeling dazzled, " I never thought of that. Well, that's a great thing. But it must be a great *responsibility too. "

---

128. əd'ventʃərəs. — 132. 'kʌrɪd. — 138. 'vɛərɪd; ɪks'pɪərɪəns. — 139. kə'rɪə. — 147. 'wɔː'rekɔːd; ɪks'kjuːz. — 150. 'ɔnəd. — 151. ə'bæʃt; sə'pouzɪŋ. — 153. 'mɔdɪst. — 154. 'prezɪdənsi. — 155. li'dʒɪtimət; æm'bɪʃn. — 156. prə'vaidɪd. — 159. ri͵spɒnsɪ'bɪlɪtɪ.

160 " It is, " said the President, looking just like his *pictures on the *campaign buttons.

" Why, it must be an *awful responsibility ! " said Johnny. " I can't hardly see how a mortal man can bear it. Tell me, Mr. President, " he said, " may I ask you a
165 question? "

" Certainly, " said the President, looking prouder and more *responsible and more and more like his picture on the campaign buttons every minute.

" Well, " said Johnny, " it sounds like a fool question, but
170 it's this : This is a great big country of ours, Mr. President, and it's got the most *amazing lot of different people in it. How can any President satisfy all those people at one time? Can you yourself, Mr. President? "

The President looked a bit taken *aback for a minute.
175 But then he gave Johnny Pye a *statesman's *glance.

" With the help of God, " he said, *solemnly, " and in *accordance with the principles of our great party, I intend—— "

But Johnny didn't even hear the end of the sentence.
180 For, even as the President was speaking, he heard a step outside in the *corridor and he knew, somehow, it wasn't the step of a *secretary or a *guard. He was glad the President had said " with the help of God " for that sort of *softened the step. And when the President finished,
185 Johnny *bowed.

" Thank you, Mr. President, " he said; " that's what I wanted to know. And now I'll go back to Martinsville, I guess. "

" Go back to Martinsville? " said the President, *sur-
190 prised.

" Yes, sir, " said Johnny. " For I don't think I'm cut out for politics. "

160. 'pɪktʃəz. — 161. kæm'peɪn. — 162. 'ɔːfl. — 167. ri'spɔn-sibl. — 171. ə'meɪzɪŋ. — 174. ə'bæk. — 175. 'steɪtsmənz; glɑːns. — 176. 'sɔləmli. — 177. ə'kɔːdəns. — 181. 'kɔrɪdɔː(r). — 182. 'se-krɪtrɪ; gɑːd. — 184. 'sɔfənd. — 185. baud. — 189. sə'praɪzd.

THE WHITE HOUSE IN WASHINGTON.

" And is that all you have to say to the President of the United States? " said his uncle-to-be, in a *fume.

195   But the President had been thinking, meanwhile, and he was a bigger man than the congressman.

" Wait a minute, congressman, " he said. " This young man's *honest, at least, and I like his looks. *Moreover, of all the people who've come to see me in the last six months,

200 he's the only one who hasn't wanted something—except the White House cat, and I guess she wanted something, too, because she *meowed. You don't want to be President, young man—and, *confidentially, I don't blame you. But how would you like to be *postmaster at Martins-

205 ville? "

" Postmaster at Martinsville? " said Johnny. "But—— "

" Oh, it's only a tenth-class post office, " said the President, " but, for once in my life, I'll do something because I want to, and let Congress yell its head off. Come—is

210 it yes or no? "

Johnny thought of all the places he'd been and all the trades he'd worked at. He thought, *queerly enough, of the old drunk fiddler dead in the ditch, but he knew he couldn't be that. Mostly, though, he thought of Martins-

215 ville and Susie Marsh. And, though he'd just heard the Fool-Killer's step, he *defied the Fool-Killer.

" Why, it's yes, of course, Mr. President, " he said, " for then I can marry Susie. "

,, That's as good a reason as you'll find, " said the Presi-

220 dent. " And now, I'll just write a note. "

194. fjuːm. — 198. ˈɔnɪst; mɔəˈrouvə. — 202 mjuːd. — 203. ˌkɔn-fɪˈdenʃəlɪ. — 204. ˈpoustmɑːstə. — 212. ˈkwɪəlɪ. — 216. dɪˈfaɪd.

NOTES

3. he'd : he would. — **4.** he'd : he had. — **5.** now and then : from time to time. — **6.** such a man (as the Fool-Killer). — **8.** kept driving him on : continued to prevent him from remaining long in the same place. — **12.** pants : (here, familiar for) trousers. — **15.** was turned : was reaching the age of; or sꝺ: approximately; scared : greatly frightened. — **17.** to ravel... out : to make clear. — **18.** tie to : attach himself to. — **28.** stuffed : filled up. — **29.** contemporaneous : adequate for solving the problems of the present time. — **32.** to run : to govern; there's : (colloquial for) there are. — **37.** right away : directly and immediately. — **38.** congressman : member of the American Parliament, called Congress and composed of the House of Representatives and the Senate; about his size : about the biggest (the highest-placed) person he could hope to interest in his case. — **40.** upstanding : well-built (physically and morally); the Republican ticket : for the Republican Party, one of the two great political parties in the United States. — **41.** sounded : appeared, when he heard it. — **42.** was after : was looking for. — **43.** a senator : a member of the Senate, or upper house of the American Parliament. — **44.** Democratic : that is the name of the other great political party. — **47.** right : exactly. — **48.** seemed to hear : thought he heard. — **50.** he'd better : it would be better for him; buckle down : set to something energetically. — **51.** he struck : he established himself. — **55.** Susie Marsh : see Part I, l. 93. — **58.** gave a jump and thump : felt jumping and thumping (beating with heavy strokes). — **65.** dry goods : (in America) haberdashery (Susie Marsh ascribes to Johnny himself all the successes of his various employers). — **66.** coughed (because he was embarrassed). — **71.** a bump : a dull-sounding knock. — **72.** but (I) never (knew) how. — **74.** how's : (colloquial for) how are. — **75.** right sudden : very suddenly. — **76.** trial : thing or event causing difficulties or pain. — **77.** gone the way of all flesh : (reference to a current phrase, and to the title of a book by Samuel Butler) died. — **79.** run down : lose its value. — **80.** likely : promising. — **87.** betwixt

and between : (the two words are synonymous) half and half, very uncertain. — **89.** turned out : became; her promise (to marry him). — **94.** uncle-to-be : Congressman Marsh, Susie's uncle. — **96.** cheerful(ly). — **97.** appointment : rendezvous. — **99.** along : with me. — **100.** dum(b)founded : confounded by surprise and emotion. — **102.** bill : law, when not yet voted by Congress; go into : speak of the details of; slick down : make smooth. — **106.** wrung : pressed strongly. — **109.** was bound to : could not fail to. — **112.** signify : matter. — **113.** take it from me : take my word for it, believe me. — **115.** trout : *truite*; saddle galls : (literally) injuries caused to a horseman by his saddle, (here, figuratively) wounds inflicted upon the President by the attacks of Congress. — **116.** to show : to become visible; feasted his eyes : looked avidly. — **118.** bother : worry, annoy. — **125.** cut in : interfered. — **127.** in season : opportunely. — **129.** settle down : establish himself. — **130.** ripe wisdom : wisdom coming from a man who has had a long experience. — **132.** curried : *étrillé* (here, the meaning of the phrase is : a little thing is quickly done). — **133.** callers : visitors. — **134.** drew out : caused to speak, willingly or no. — **139.** obvious : evident, evidently adequate. — **140.** slapped : struck. — **143.** rightly fitted : having the exact abilities. — **145.** thoughtful : pensive; with mine : to write mine. — **147.** war-record : statement of war-services; Excuse me : (for exclaiming : Hell ! which is not polite). — **148.** He's worth : he can gain. — **151.** abashed : made timid. — **156.** provided : on condition. — **157.** dazzled : almost blinded by excessive brightness. — **161.** campaign buttons : during the President's electoral campaign, his enthusiastic supporters had worn buttons with his picture on them. — **163.** can't : can.

— **169.** fool : foolish. — **170.** of ours : in which we live. — **171.** amazing : astonishing. — **172.** at one time : at the same time. — **174.** taken aback : disconcerted. — **175.** gave... glance : looked at Johnny majestically. — **183.** sort of softened : made rather less loud. — **185.** bowed : *s'inclina.* — **188.** guess : think. — **191.** cut out : made (by nature). — **194.** fume : great anger. — **196.** bigger : greater, more intelligent. — **198.** looks : appearance. — **201.** White House : the official Residence of the President. — **202.** to meow (or mew) : *miauler.* — **204.** postmaster : master (or director) of the post-office. — **209.** yell its head off : to yell is to shout, like a dog; yell its head off means : yell till one loses one's head; here the meaning is : let Congress express its disapproval violently until it is tired. — **211.** he'd been (to or in). — **219.** as good a reason as : the best reason. — **220.** write a note (concerning Johnny's appointment to the post-office).

THÈME D'IMITATION

Le Président des États-Unis d'Amérique.

Essayons de définir le rôle du Président. Un futur Président devient d'abord membre du Congrès, quoi qu'il ait fait d'autre avant le début de sa carrière politique. Le courage et la ténacité sont les qualités dont il a le plus besoin. Il doit continuer pendant des années entières à faire des efforts pour gagner la confiance et l'estime des électeurs. Tôt ou tard, il se dira peut-être qu'il n'est pas le plus heureux des hommes, et que ce qu'il a obtenu n'est pas exactement ce qu'il cherchait. Mais sa situation, qui devient de plus en plus difficile d'année en année, est une des plus importantes du monde, et possède, aux yeux des petits garçons américains, un prestige éblouissant.

VERSION AVEC QUESTIONS

American politics in the 19th century.

Of the two great parties which at this hour almost share the nation between them, I should say that one has the best cause, and the other contains the best men. The philosopher, the poet, or the religious man, will of course wish to cast his vote with the democrat, for free-trade, for wide suffrage, for the abolition of legal cruelties in the penal code, and for facilitating in every manner the access of the young and the poor to the sources of wealth and power. But he can rarely accept the persons whom the so-called popular party propose to him as representatives of these liberalities. They have not at heart the ends which give to the name of democracy what hope and virtue are in it. The spirit of our American radicalism is destructive and aimless : it is not loving; it has no ulterior and divine ends, but is destructive only out of hatred and selfishness. On the other side, the conservative party, composed of the most moderate, able, and cultivated part of the population, is timid, and merely defensive of property. It vindicates no right, it aspires to no real good, it brands no crime, it proposes no generous policy; it does not build, nor write, nor cherish the arts, nor foster religion, nor establish schools, nor encourage science, nor emancipate the slave, nor befriend the poor, or the Indian, or the immigrant. From neither party, when in power, has the world any benefit to expect in science, art, or humanity, at all commensurate with the resources of the nation.

R. W. EMERSON, Essays.

QUESTIONS : 1. *For which of the two parties described above do you think the author would have voted in an election? Give your reasons.* — 2. *If a member of each party had read this text, who have disliked it most? Give your reasons.* — 3. *Do you think this text would have reminded Johnny of the Fool-Killer?*

QUESTIONNAIRE

When did Johnny begin to forget about the Fool-Killer? — How did the Fool-Killer still trouble him? — What happened when Johnny tried book-learning? — Why did he go to Washington? — Why didn't he try and see the President himself? — Whom did he see? — What answers did he get? — Was he satisfied? — What was his next job? — Whose arrival made a change in his life? — How did Susie sum up Johnny's career? — What had happened to the miller and the mill? — Try and sum up the story of Johnny's love for Susie? — Why do you think the Fool-Killer objected to Johnny's love? — Why was Johnny glad to see the President? — How did the President get Johnny to tell his story? — What career did he suggest to him? — What arguments did Susie's uncle mention in favour of that career? — What questions did Johnny ask of the President before he made up his mind? — What was his final decision, and why? — Why did the President offer a post-office to Johnny? — Why did Johnny accept it?

INTONATION

(Émotionnelle, ascendante, sous-entendu ironique.)

24. and that was \frequent ↑

(Émotionnelle, descendante, affirmation emphatique.)

70. \I never thought you were a fool ‖

(Neutre, ascendante, question appelant la réponse par oui ou par non.)

164. ⁻May I ⁻ask you a ₋question ↑

(Neutre, descendante, affirmation simple.)

220. and ⁻now, I'll ⁻just ⁻write a \note ‖

III. JOHNNY'S ENCOUNTERS
WITH THE SCISSORS-GRINDER

Well, he was as good as his word, and Johnny and his
Susie were *married and went back to live in Martinsville.
And, as soon as Johnny learned the ways of *postmastering,
he found it as good a trade as most.   There wasn't much
mail in Martinsville, but, in between whiles, he ran the mill, 5
and that was a good trade too.   And all the time, he knew,
at the back of his mind, that he hadn't quite settled
*accounts with the Fool-Killer.   But he didn't much care
about that, for he and Susie were happy.   And after a
while they had a child, and that was the most *remarkable 10
experience that had ever happened to any young couple,
though the doctor said it was a *perfectly normal *baby.
One evening, when his son was about a year old, Johnny
Pye took the river road, going home.   It was a *mite longer
than the hill road, but it was the cool of the evening, and 15
there's times when a man likes to walk by himself, fond as
he may be of his wife and family.
He was thinking of the way things had turned out for
him, and they seemed to him pretty astonishing and *singular, as they do to most folks, when you think them over. 20
In fact, he was thinking so hard that, before he knew it,
he'd almost stumbled over an old *scissors-*grinder who'd
set up his grindstone and tools by the side of the road.   The
scissors-grinder had his cart with him, but he'd turned the
horse out to graze—and a lank, old, white horse it was, 25
with every rib showing.   And he was very busy, putting an
edge on a *scythe.

2. 'mærid. — 3. 'poustmɑːstəriŋ. — 8. ə'kaunts. — 10. ri'maː-
kəbl. — 12. 'pəːfiktli; 'beibi. — 14. mait. — 19. 'siŋgjulə. —
22. 'sizəz; 'graində. — 27. saiठ.

THE OUTSIDE OF THE POST-OFFICE
IN A SMALL AMERICAN TOWN, LIKE MARTINSVILLE.

THE INSIDE
OF A SMALL AMERICAN POST-OFFICE.

"Oh, sorry," said Johnny Pye. "I didn't know anybody was camping here. But you might come round to
30   my house tomorrow—my wife's got some knives that need
*sharpening."

Then he stopped, for the old man gave him a long, keen
look.

"Why, it's you, Johnny Pye," said the old man. "And
35   how do you do, Johnny Pye! You've been a long time
coming—in fact, now and then, I thought I'd have to fetch
you. But you're here at last."

Johnny Pye was a grown man now, but he began to
tremble.

40   "But it isn't you?" he said, *wildly. "I mean you're
not him! Why, I've known how he looks all my life!
He's a big man, with a checked shirt, and he carries a
hickory stick with a lump of lead in one end."

"Oh, no," said the scissors-grinder, *quite *quiet.
45   "You may have thought of me that way, but that's not the
way I am." And Johnny Pye heard the scythe go whet-
whet-whet on the stone. The old man ran some water
on it and looked at the edge. Then he shook his head as
if the edge didn't quite satisfy him. "Well, Johnny, are
50   you ready?" he said, after a while.

"Ready?" said Johnny, in a *hoarse voice. "Of
course I'm not ready."

"That's what they all say," said the old man, nodding
his head, and the scythe went whet-whet on the stone.
55   Johnny wiped his *brow and started to *argue it out.

"You see, if you'd found me earlier," he said, "or
later. I don't want to be *unreasonable, but I've got a
wife and a child."

"Most has wives and many has children," said the old
60   man, grimly, and the scythe went whet-whet on the stone
as he pushed the *treadle. And a shower of sparks flew,
very clear and bright, for the night had begun to fall.

---

31. ʃɑːpənɪŋ. — 40. 'waildlɪ. — 44. kwait; kwaɪit. — 51. hɔːs. —
55. qrau; 'ɑːgjuː. — 57. ʌnˈriːznəbl. — 61. tredl.

" Oh, stop that damn racket and let a man think for a minute ! " said Johnny, *desperate.   " I can't go, I tell you I won't. It isn't time. It's—— "   65

The old man stopped the grindstone and pointed with the scythe at Johnny Pye.

" Tell me one good reason, " he said. " There's men would be missed in the world, but are you one of them? A clever man might be missed, but are you a clever man? "   70

" No, " said Johnny, thinking of the herb doctor. " I had a chance to be clever, but I gave it up. "

" One, " said the old man, ticking off on his fingers. " Well, a rich man might be missed—by some. But you aren't rich, I take it. "   75

" No, " said Johnny, thinking of the merchant, " nor wanted to be. "

" Two, " said the old man. " Cleverness—riches— they're done. But there's still *martial *bravery and being a *hero. There might be an *argument to make, if you 80 were one of those. "

Johnny Pye shuddered a little, remembering the way that battlefield had looked, out West, when the Indians were dead and the fight over.

" No, " he said, " I've fought, but I'm not a hero. "   85

" Well, then, there's *religion, " said the old man, sort of *patient, " and *science, and—but what's the use? We know what you did with those. I might feel a trifle of *compunction if I had to deal with a President of the United States. But—— "   90

" Oh, you know well enough I ain't President, " said Johnny, with a groan. " Can't you get it over with and be done? "

" You're not putting up a very good case, " said the old man, shaking his head. " I'm surprised at you, Johnny. 95 Here you spend your youth running away from being a fool. And yet, what's the first thing you do, when you're man

---

64. 'despərət. — 79. 'mɑːʃəl; 'breɪvrɪ. — 80. 'hɪərou; 'ɑːgjumənt — 86. rɪ'lɪdʒən. — 87. 'peɪʃənt; 'saɪəns. — 89. kəm'pʌŋkʃən.

grown? Why, you marry a girl, settle down in your home
town, and start raising children when you don't know
100 how they'll turn out. You might have known I'd catch up
with you, then—you just put yourself in my way. "

" Fool I may be, " said Johnny Pye in his *agony, " and
if you take it like that, I guess we're all fools. But Susie's my
wife, and my child's my child. And, as for work in the
105 world—well, somebody has to be postmaster, or folks
wouldn't get the mail. "

" Would it matter much if they didn't? " said the old
man, pointing his scythe.

" Well, no, I don't suppose it would, considering what's
110 on the post cards, " said Johnny Pye. " But while it's my
business to sort it, I'll sort it as well as I can. "

The old man whetted his scythe so hard that a long
shower of sparks flew out on the grass.

" Well," he said, " I've got my job, too, and I do it
115 *likewise. But I'll tell you what I'll do. You're coming my
way, no doubt of it, but, looking you over, you don't look
quite ripe yet. So I'll let you off for a while. For that
matter, " said he, " if you'll answer one question of mine
—how a man can be a human being and not be a fool—I'll
120 let you off *permanent. It'll be the first time in *history, "
he said, " but you've got to do something on your own
hook, once in a while. And now you can walk along,
Johnny Pye. "

With that he ground the scythe till the sparks flew out
125 like the tail of a *comet and Johnny Pye walked along.
The air of the *meadow had never seemed so sweet to him
before.

All the same, even with his *relief, he didn't quite forget,
and sometimes Susie had to tell the children not to *disturb
130 father because he was thinking. But time went ahead, as it
does, and pretty soon Johnny Pye found he was forty.
He'd never expected to be forty, when he was young, and

102. 'ægəni. — 115. 'laɪkwaɪz. — 120. 'pəːmənənt; 'histərɪ. —
125. 'kɔmɪt. — 126. 'medou. — 128. rɪ'liːf. — 129. dɪ'stəːb.

it kind of surprised him. But there it was, though he couldn't say he felt much different, except now and then when he stooped over. And he was a solid *citizen of the 135 town, well-liked and well-respected, with a growing family and a stake in the *community, and when he thought those things over, they kind of surprised him too. But, pretty soon, it was as if things had always been that way.

It was after his eldest son had been *drowned out fishing 140 that Johnny Pye met the scissors-grinder again. But this time, he was bitter and *distracted, and, if he could have got to the old man, he'd have done him a mortal harm. But, somehow or other, when he tried to come to grips with him, it was like reaching for air and mist. He could see the 145 sparks fly from the ground scythe, but he couldn't even touch the wheel.

" You *coward ! " said Johnny Pye. " Stand up and fight like a man ! " But the old man just nodded his head and the wheel kept grinding and grinding. 150

" Why couldn't you have taken me? " said Johnny Pye, as if those words had never been said before. " What's the sense in all this? Why can't you take me now? "

Then he tried to *wrench the scythe from the old man's hands, but he couldn't touch it. And then he fell down 155 and lay on the grass for a while.

" Time passes, " said the old man, nodding his head. " Time passes. "

" It will never *cure the *grief I have for my son, " said Johnny Pye. 160

" It will not, " said the old man, nodding his head. " But time passes. Would you leave your wife a widow and your other children fatherless for the sake of your grief? "

" No, God help me ! " said Johnny Pye. " That 165 wouldn't be right for a man. "

" Then go home to your house, Johnny Pye, " said the

---

135. 'sɪtɪzən. — 137. kə'mjuːnɪtɪ. — 140. draund. — 142. dɪ-'stræktɪd. — 148. kauəd. — 154. renʃ. — 159. kjuə; griːf.

old man. And Johnny Pye went, but there were lines in his face that hadn't been there before.

170   And time passed, like the flow of the river, and Johnny Pye's children married and had houses and children of their own. And Susie's hair grew white, and her back grew bent, and when Johnny Pye and his children followed her to her grave, folks said she'd died in the fullness of years, but
175 that was hard for Johnny Pye to believe. Only folks didn't talk as plain as they used to, and the sun didn't heat as much, and sometimes, before dinner, he'd go to sleep in his chair.

And once, after Susie had died, the President of those days
180 came through Martinsville and Johnny Pye shook hands with him and there was a piece in the paper about his shaking hands with two Presidents, fifty years apart. Johnny Pye cut out the clipping and kept it in his pocket-book. He liked this President all right, but, as he told
185 people, he wasn't a patch on the other one fifty years ago. Well, you couldn't expect it—you didn't have Presidents these days, not to call them Presidents. All the same, he took a lot of *satisfaction in the clipping.

He didn't get down to the river road much any more—it
190 wasn't too long a walk, of course, but he just didn't often feel like it. But, one day, he slipped away from the *grand-daughter that was taking care of him, and went. It was kind of a steep road, really—he didn't remember its being so steep.
195   " Well ", said the scissors-grinder, " and good afternoon to you, Johnny Pye. "

" You'll have to talk a little louder, " said Johnny Pye. " My *hearing's perfect, but folks don't speak as plain as they used to. *Stranger in town? "
200   " Oh, so that's the way it is, " said the scissors-grinder.

" Yes, that's the way it is, " said Johnny Pye. He knew he ought to be *afraid of this fellow, now he'd put on his

---

188. ˌsætis'fækʃən. — 191. 'grænddɔːtə. — 198. 'hɪərɪŋz. — 199. 'streɪnʒə. — 202. ə'freɪd.

spectacles and got a good look at him, but, for the life of him, he couldn't remember why.

" I know just who you are, " he said, a little *fretfully.   205
" Never forgot a face in my life, and your name's right on the tip of my tongue—— "   \

" Oh, don't bother about names, " said the scissors-grinder. " We're old *acquaintances. And I asked you a question, years ago—do you remember that? "   210

" Yes, " said Johnny Pye, " I remember. " Then he began to laugh—a high, old man's laugh.—" And of all the fool questions I ever was asked, " he said, " that certainly took the cake. "

" Oh? " said the scissors-grinder.   215

" *Uh-huh, " said Johnny Pye. " For you asked me how a man could be a human being and yet not be a fool. And the answer is—when he's dead and gone and *buried. Any fool would know that. "

" That so? " said the scissors-grinder.   220

" Of course, " said Johnny Pye. " I ought to know. I'll be ninety-two next *November, and I've shook hands with two Presidents. The first President I shook—— "

"I'll be interested to hear about that," said the scissors-grinder, " but we've got a little business, first. For, if all   225
human beings are fools, how does the world get ahead? "

" Oh, there's lots of other things, " said Johnny Pye, kind of impatient. " There's the brave and the wise and the clever —and they're apt to roll it ahead as much as an inch. But it's all mixed in together. For, Lord, it's only   230
some fool kind of creature that would have *crawled out of the sea to dry land in the first place—or got dropped from ⸌ the Garden of *Eden, if you like it better that way. You can't depend on the kind of folks people think they are— you've got to go by what they do. And I wouldn't give   235
much for a man that some folks hadn't thought was a fool, in his time. "

205. 'fretfuli. — 209. ə'kweintənsız. — 216. 'ju:'hju. — 218. 'berıd. — 222. no'vembə. — 231. krɔːld. — 233. 'iːdən.

"Well," said the scissors-grinder, "you've answered my question—at least as well as you could, which is all you can

240 *expect of a man. So I'll keep my part of the *bargain. "

"And what was that? " said Johnny. " For, while it's all straight in my head, I don't quite *recollect the details."

"Why," said the scissors-grinder, rather testy, " I'm to let you go, you old fool ! You'll never see me again till

245 the Last *Judgment. There'll be trouble in the *office about it, " said he, " but you've got to do what you like, once in a while. "

" *Phew ! " said Johnny Pye. " That needs thinking over ! " And he *scratched his head.

250 " Why? " said the scissors-grinder, a bit *affronted. " It ain't often I offer a man *eternal life. "

" Well, " said Johnny Pye, " I take it very kind, but, you see, it's this way. " He thought for a *moment. " No, " he said, " you wouldn't understand. You can't have touched

255 seventy yet, by your looks, and no young man would. "

" Try me, " said the scissors-grinder.

" Well, " said Johnny Pye. " It's this way, " and he scratched his head again. " I'm not saying—if you'd made the offer forty years ago, or even twenty. But,

260 well, now, let's just take one *detail. Let's say " 'teeth'. "

" Wel l, of course," said the scissors-grinder, " *naturally—I mean you could hardly expect me to do anything about that. "

" I thought so, " said Johnny Pye. " Well, you see,

265 these are good, *bought teeth, but I'm sort of tired of hearing them click. And spectacles, I suppose, the same? "

" I'm afraid so, " said the scissors-grinder. " I can't *interfere with time, you know—that's not my *department. And, frankly, you couldn't expect, at a hundred and eighty,

---

240. ıks'p ekt; 'bɑːgin. — 242. ˌrekə'lekt. — 245. 'dʒʌdʒmənt; ɔfıs. — 248. fjuː. — 249. skrætʃt. — 250. ə'frʌntid. — 251. ı'təːnl. — 253. 'moumənt. — 260. 'diːteil. — 261. 'nætʃərəli. — 265. bɔːt. — 268. 'ıntəfıə; dı'pɑːtmənt.

let's say, to be quite the man you was at ninety. But still, 270
you'd be a wonder ! "

" Maybe so, " said Johnny Pye, " but, you see—well, the
truth is, I'm an old man now. You wouldn't think it to
look at me, but it's so. And my friends—well, they're
gone—and Susie and the boy—and somehow you don't 275
get as close to the younger people, except the children.
And to keep on just going and going till Judgment Day,
with nobody around to talk to that had real horse sense—
well, no, sir, it's a *handsome offer but I just don't feel up
to *accepting it. It may not be *patriotic of me, and I feel 280
sorry for Martinsville. It'd do wonders for the climate
and the *chamber of *commerce to have a leading citizen
live till Judgment Day. But a man's got to do as he likes,
at least once in his life. " He stopped and looked at the
scissors-grinder. " I'll admit, I'd kind of like to beat out 285
*Ike *Leavis, " he said. " To hear him talk, you'd think
nobody had ever pushed ninety before. But I suppose——"

" I'm afraid we can't issue a *limited *policy, " said the
scissors-grinder.

" Well, " said Johnny Pye, " I just thought of it. And 290
Ike's all right. " He waited a moment. " Tell me, " he
said, in a low voice. "Well, you know what I mean.
*Afterwards. I mean, if you're likely to see."—he *coughed
—" your friends again. I mean, if it's so—like some folks
believe. "

" I can't tell you that, " said the scissors-grinder. " I 295
only go so far. "

" Well, there's no harm in asking, " said Johnny Pye,
rather humbly. He *peered into the darkness; a last
*shower of sparks flew from the scythe, then the *whir of 300
the wheel stopped.

" H'm, " said Johnny Pye, testing the edge. " That's
a well-ground scythe. But they used to grind'em better

---

279. 'hænsəm. — 280. ək'septiŋ; pætri'ɔtik. — 282. 'tʃeimbə;
'kɔməːs. — 286. aik; 'levis. — 288. 'limitid; 'pɔlisi. — 293. 'aːftə-
wədz; kɔːft. — 299. piəd. — 300. ʃauə; (h)wəː.

in the old days. " He listened and looked, for a moment,
305 anxiously.

" Oh, *Lordy ! " he said. " There's *Helen coming
to look for me. She'll take me back to the house. "

" Not this time, " said the scissors-grinder. " Yes,
there isn't bad steel in that scythe. Well, let's go, Johnny
310 Pye. "

306. 'lɔ:di; 'helən.

NOTES

1. was as good as : kept. — **3.** the ways of postmastering : the functions of a postmaster. — **5.** in between whiles : in the intervals; ran : managed. — **14.** a mite longer : longer by a very short distance. — **15.** the cool (part, or moment) of the evening. — **16.** there *are* times; by himself : alone; fond as he may be : however fond he may be. — **18.** turned out : come to be. — **19.** pretty : rather. — **20.** think them over : reflect about them. — **21.** so hard : so deeply. — **22.** stumbled over : knocked accidentally against; grinder : *repasseur*. — **23.** grindstone : *meule*. — **24.** Turned... out : detached from the cart. — **25.** graze : feed on grass; lank : tall and lean. — **26.** showing : visible; putting an edge on : making sharp. — **32.** keen : penetrating. — **36.** I'd have : I would be obliged. — **38.** a grown man : a grown-up. — **41.** him : the Fool-Killer. — **45.** that way : so. — **46.** go whet-whet-whet : make that noise (whet-whet) when the edge was rubbing against the grindstone (to whet is to sharpen). — **47.** ran : dropped. — **51.** hoarse : made rough by anxiety. — **55.** brow : forehead; to argue it out : to discuss the point to the end. — **59.** has : have. — **60.** grimly : severely. — **61.** treadle : lever moved by foot and imparting motion to machine; shower : heavy rain. — **63.** racket : unpleasant noise; a man : (indefinite) people (in fact : me). — **68.** there *are* men *who* would be missed : whose absence would be regretted. — **72.** gave it up : let it go. — **73.** ticking off : marking numbers. — **74.** by some : not by everybody. — **75.** I take it : I suppose. — **76.** nor : and I have not. — **79.** done : finished. — **82.** shuddered : trembled, as with fear. — **83.** out West : far in the West. — **84.** over : finished. — **88.** trifle : small quantity or degree. — **89.** compunction : remorse or scruple. — **92.** get it over with and be done : (familiar for) have finished quickly. — **94.** putting up a case : presenting a case, as before a tribunal. — **98.** home town : native town. — **100.** catch up with you : (vulgar for) catch you. — **102.** agony : intense suffering or anxiety. — **107.** matter much : have much importance; didn't (get the mail). — **111.** sort : *trier*. — **115.** likewise : similarly. — **116.** looking you over : when I examine you. — **117.** let you off : let you escape; for that matter : and, indeed. — **120.** permanent*ly*. — **121.** on your own hook : on your own account, for your own pleasure. — **122.** once in a while : now and again. — **130.** went ahead : advanced. — **133.** there it was : it had indeed happened. —**135.** stooped over : bent forward. — **137.** a stake in the community : a personal interest and part in its life. — **140.** out fishing : when he was fishing in a boat. — **142.** distracted : out of himself, almost mad; got to : reached. — **144.** to come to grips with : to grasp in close combat. — **145.** to reach for : to try and reach. — **154.** to wrench : to take by violence. — **159.** cure : remedy; grief : sorrow. — **163.** for the sake of : because of. — **168.** lines : wrinkles. — **176.** plain : clearly. — **183.** clipping : a piece cut from a newspaper. — **185.** wasn't a patch on : could not bear comparison with. — **188.** a lot of : much. — **191.** feel like it : feel tempted to act that way; slipped : went furtively. — **199.** stranger : one who is not a regular inhabitant. — **203.** for the life of him : even if his life had depended on it. — **205.** fretfully : nervously. — **208.** bother : be troubled. — **212.** high : high-toned, shrill. — **213.** fool(ish). — **214.** took the cake : won the prize, beat the others. — **216.** uh-huh : onomatopoeia representing old Johnny's laughter. — **220.** (Is) that so ? — **222.** shook : (incorrect for) shaken. — **226.** get ahead : advance. — **227.** there *are*. — **229.** to roll it ahead : to make it advance. — **231.** crawled : moved slowly, like a reptile. — **232.** got dropped : deserved to be expelled. — **233.** If you like it better that way : Johnny offers the scissors-grinder the choice between two different explanations of the early history of mankind, the second being the Christian version of things. — **234.** depend on the kind of folks people think they are : judge people safely according to their own view of themselves. — **235.** to go by : to determine your judgment according to. — **236.** that

some folks hadn't thought was a fool : that had not been considered as a fool by some people. — **239.** all you can : all *one* can. — **240.** keep my part of the bargain : fulfil my engagement. — **242.** straight : clear and correct. — **243.** testy : testily, irritably. — **245.** in the office : the Fool-Killer is here supposed to belong to some supernatural administration, of which he is only an executive. — **246.** you've got to do what you like : one must do what one likes. — **248.** phew : an interjection of surprise and disgust. — **250.** affronted : feeling insulted. — **251.** ain't : isn't. — **252.** Take it very kind (ly) : take it as a great kindness. — **254.** touched : reached. — **255.** by your looks : judging by your appearance; would (understand). — **266.** click : make a small metallic noise. — **267.** so : it would be so. — **270.** you was : you were. — **276.** as close to : as intimate with. — **278.** around : near us; horse sense : good common sense. — **279.** feel up to : feel able to. — **281.** It'd do wonders for the climate : it would be an excellent advertisement for the climate. — **287.** pushed : passed. — **288.** issue a limited policy : (like an insurance policy) give you a guarantee of life for a limited number of years. — **291.** all right : in good health. — **293.** if you're likely to see : if it is probable that you (one) will see. — **294.** like : (vulgar for) as. — **296.** I only go so far : I only go as far as death, and not beyond. — **299.** peered : looked attentively. — **300.** whir : steady noise, as of engine. — **302.** testing : feeling. — **306.** Lordy : a mild interjection; Helen : Johnny's grand-daughter, from whom he had slipped away. — **309.** there isn't bad steel in that scythe : as the steel is good, it will do its work efficiently (its work being the Foll-Killer's job of killing Fools).

THÈME D'IMITATION

Le retour du voyageur.

« Dès que mon voyage sera fini », avait promis Watson à ses amis, « je vous raconterai mes aventures. » Il tint parole, et commença, le premier soir, à décrire sa traversée; puis il leur dit : « J'ai mis du temps à visiter Paris, mais je n'ai pas oublié un seul monument important. J'ai fait de mon mieux pour vous satisfaire, et je n'ai pas voulu compter sur mes souvenirs. Voici donc de nombreuses photographies ». Et, pendant plusieurs soirées, il continua à leur montrer des images de la capitale française. Quant à la campagne de notre pays, il ne la connaissait pas aussi bien. Mais cela avait-il beaucoup d'importance ? C'était le charme magique de Paris qui intéressait les amis de Watson.

VERSION AVEC QUESTIONS

On the fear of death.

Perhaps the best cure for the fear of death is to reflect that life has a beginning as well as an end. There was a time when we were not : this gives us no concern — why, then, should it trouble us that a time will come when we shall cease to be ? I have no wish to have been alive a hundred years ago, or in the reign of Queen Anne : why should I regret and lay it so much to heart that I shall not be alive a hundred years hence, in the reign of I cannot tell whom ?

To die is only to be as we were before we were born; yet no one feels any remorse, or regret, or repugnance, in contemplating this last idea. It is rather a relief and disburthening of the mind : it seems to have been holiday-time with us then : we were not called to appear upon the stage of life, to wear robes or tatters, to laugh or cry, be hooted or applauded; we had lain *perdus* all this while, snug, out of harm's way; and had slept out our thousands of centuries without wanting to be waked up; at peace and free from care, in a sleep deeper and calmer than that of infancy, wrapped in the softest and finest dust. And the worst that we dread is, after a short, fretful, feverish being, after vain hopes and idle fears, to sink to final repose again, and forget the troubled dream of life!...

William HAZLITT, Table-Talk.

QUESTIONS : 1. *Would you like to have been alive in the reign of Louis XIV? — 2. Judging from this text, does Hazlitt like this life? — 3. Is the expression " the dream of life " original ? And what does it suggest to you?*

QUESTIONNAIRE

When were Johnny and Susie married? — What did Johnny think of postmastering? — How did he increase his income? — What did Susie and he think of their child? — Did the doctor agree with them? — Why did Johnny take the river road? — Describe the scissors-grinder. His tools. His horse. — Who was this scissors-grinder? — Why was Johnny surprised when he understood this identity? — Was the sound of the scythe pleasant to Johnny? — How did the scissors-grinder work his grindstone? — What sort of people was he ready to spare? — What did he reproach Johnny with having done ? — What did he think of Johnny's excuse for his professional employment? — What question did he ask before he let Johnny go? — What was Johnny's position when he was forty? — When did he meet with the scissors-grinder again? — What took place between them this second time? — What lesson did the scissors-grinder teach to Johnny? — Was Susie still young when she died? — What was the clipping kept by Johnny about ? — Did Johnny recognize the scissors-grinder when he saw him for the third time ? — Did he admit that his faculties had become weaker? — How did he answer the fatal question? — And what was his view on the world in general? — What did the scissors-grinder offer to Johnny? — Was he authorized by his superiors to make such an offer? — How did Johnny receive that offer? — And why? — What could have tempted Johnny to accept the offer ? — What were his feelings to Ike Leavis? — What troubled him at the last moment? — Did Helen take him home after his last encounter with the scissors-grinder?

INTONATION

(Neutre, ascendante, sous-entendu ironique.)
35. you've been a ⁻long time _coming ↑

(Neutre, ascendante, question appelant réponse oui ou non.)
70. ⁻Are you a _clever ╱ man? ↑ .

(Émotionnelle, descendante, affirmation emphatique.)
119. I'll let you off ╲permanent ‖

(Neutre, descendante, affirmation simple.)
248. ⁻that −needs −thinking ╲ over ‖

BY THE WATERS OF BABYLON

I. THE JOURNEY EAST TOWARDS THE CITY OF THE GODS

The north and the west and the south are good hunting ground, but it is *forbidden to go east. It is forbidden to go to any of the Dead Places *except to search for *metal and then he who touches the metal must be a priest or the son of a priest. *Afterwards, both the man 5 and the metal must be *purified. These are the rules and the laws; they are well made. It is forbidden to cross the great river and look upon the place that was the Place of the Gods—this is most strictly forbidden. We do not even say its name though we know its name. It is there that 10 spirits live, and *demons—it is there that there are the *ashes of the Great Burning. These things are forbidden—they have been forbidden since the beginning of time.

My father is a priest; I am the son of a priest. I have been in the Dead Places near us, with my father—at first, I was 15 *afraid. When my father went into the house to search for the metal, I stood by the door and my heart felt small and weak. It was a dead man's house, a spirit house. It did not have the smell of man, though there were old bones in a corner. But it is not fitting that a priest's son should 20 show fear. I looked at the bones in the *shadow and kept my voice still.

2. fə'bidən. — 3. ik'sept. — 4. 'metl. — 5. 'ɑːftəwədz. — 6. 'pjuərifaid. — 11. 'diːmənz. — 12. 'æʃiz. — 16. ə'freid. — 21. 'ʃædou.

Then my father came out with the metal—a good, strong
piece. He looked at me with both eyes but I had not run
25 away. He gave me the metal to hold—I took it and did not
die. So he knew that I was truly his son and would be a
priest in my time. That was when I was very young—
*nevertheless, my brothers would not have done it, though
they are good hunters. After that, they gave me the good
30 piece of meat and the warm corner by the fire. My father
*watched over me—he was glad that I should be a priest.
But when I *boasted or wept without a reason, he punished
me more strictly than my brothers. That was right.

After a time, I myself was *allowed to go into the dead
35 houses and search for metal. So I learned the ways of
those houses—and if I saw bones, I was no longer afraid.
The bones are light and old—sometimes they will fall into
dust if you touch them. But that is a great sin.

I was *taught the *chants and the spells—I was taught
40 how to stop the running of blood from a wound and many
*secrets. A priest must know many secrets—that was what
my father said. If the hunters think we know all things
by chants and spells, they may believe so—it does not hurt
them. I was taught how to read in the old books and how
45 to make the old writings—that was hard and took a long
time. My *knowledge made me happy—it was like a fire
in my heart. Most of all, I liked to hear of the Old Days and
the stories of the gods. I asked myself many *questions
that I could not *answer, but it was good to ask them. At
50 night, I would lie *awake and listen to the wind—it seemed
to me that it was the voice of the gods as they *flew through
the air.

We are not *ignorant like the Forest People—our women
spin *wool on the wheel, our priests wear a white robe. We
55 do not eat grubs from the tree, we have not *forgotten the

28. ˌnevəðə'les. — 31. wɔtʃt. — 32. ˏ'boustid. — 34. ə'laud. —
39. tɔːt; tʃɑːnts. — 41. 'siːkrits. — 46. 'nɔlidʒ. — 48. 'kwestʃənz. —
49. 'ɑːnsə. — 50. ə'weik. — 51. fluː. — 53. 'ignərənt. — 54. wul.
—55. fə'gɔtən.

GOING INTO THE PLACE OF THE GODS TO-DAY.

old writings, although they are hard to understand. Nevertheless, my knowledge and my lack of knowledge burned in me —I wished to know more. When I was a man at last, I came to my father and said : " It is time for me to go
60 on my *journey. Give me your leave. "

He looked at me for a long time, stroking his *beard, then he said at last : " Yes, it is time. " That night, in the house of the priesthood, I asked for and *received *purification. My body hurt but my spirit was a cool
65 stone. It was my father himself who questioned me about my dreams.

He bade me look into the smoke of the fire and see—I saw and told what I saw. It was what I have always seen— a river, and, beyond it, a great Dead Place and in it the gods
70 *walking. I have always thought about that. His eyes were stern when I told him—he was no longer my father but a priest. He said : " This is a strong dream. "

" It is mine, " I said, while the smoke waved and my head felt light. They were singing the Star song in the
75 outer chamber and it was like the *buzzing of bees in my head.

He asked me how the gods were dressed, and I told him how they were dressed. We know how they were dressed from the book, but I saw them as if they were before me.
80 When I had finished, he threw the sticks three times and studied them as they fell.

" This is a very strong dream, " he said. " It may eat you up. "

" I am not afraid, " I said, and looked at him with both
85 eyes. My voice sounded thin in my ears, but that was because of the smoke.

He touched me on the breast and the forehead. He gave me the *bow and the three *arrows.

" Take them " he said, " it is forbidden to travel east.
90 It is forbidden to cross the river. It is forbidden to go to

60. 'dʒəːnɪ. — 61. bɪəd. — 63. rɪ'siːvd. — 64. ˌpjuərɪfɪ'keiʃən. — 70. 'wɔːkɪŋ. — 75. 'bʌzɪŋ. — 88. bou; 'ӕrouz.

the Place of the Gods. All these things are forbidden. "
" All these things are forbidden, " I said, but it was my
voice that spoke and not my spirit. He looked at me again.
" My son, " he said. " Once I had young dreams. If
your dreams do not eat you up, you may be a great priest,   95
If they eat you, you are still my son. Now go on your
journey. "
I went fasting, as is the law. My body hurt but not my
heart. When the dawn came, I was out of sight of the
village. I prayed and purified myself, waiting for a *sign.   100
The sign was an eagle. It flew east.
Sometimes signs are sent by bad spirits. I waited again
on the flat rock, fasting, taking no food. I was very still—I
could feel the sky above me and the earth *beneath. I
waited till the sun was beginning to sink. Then three deer   105
passed in the valley, going east—they did not wind me or see
me. There was a white *fawn with them—a very great
sign.
I *followed them, at a distance, waiting for what would
happen. My heart was troubled about going east, yet I   110
knew that I must go. My head hummed with my fasting—I
did not even see the *panther spring upon the white fawn.
But, before I knew it, the bow was in my hand. I *shouted
and the panther lifted his head from the fawn. It is not
easy to kill a panther with one arrow but the arrow went   115
through his eye and into his brain. He died as he tried to
spring—he rolled over, *tearing at the ground. Then I
knew I was meant to go east—I knew that was my journey.
When the night came, I made my fire and roasted meat.
It is eight suns journey to the east, and a man passes by·   120
many Dead Places. The Forest People are afraid of them
but I am not. Once I made my fire on the edge of a Dead
Place at night and, next morning, in the dead house, I
found a good knife, little *rusted. That was small to what
came afterward but it made my heart feel big. Always   125

---

100. sain. — 104. bi′nɪːθ. — 107. fɔːn. — 109. ′fɔloud. —
112. ′pœnθə. — 113. ′ʃautid. — 117. ′teəriŋ. — 124. ′rʌstid.

when I looked for game, it was in front of my arrow, and
twice I passed hunting parties of the Forest People without
their knowing. So I knew my magic was strong and my
journey clean, in spite of the law.

130   Toward the setting of the eighth sun, I came to the banks
of the great river. It was half a day's journey after I had left
the god-road—we do not use the god-roads now for they
are falling *apart into great blocks of stone, and the forest is
safer going. A long way off, I had seen the water through

135 trees, but the trees were thick. At last, I came out upon
an open place at the top of a cliff. There was the great
river *below, like a *giant in the sun. It is very long, very
wide. It could eat all the streams we know and still be
*thirsty. Its name is *Ou-dis-sun, the *Sacred, the Long.

140 No man of my tribe had seen it, not even my father, the
priest. It was magic and I prayed.

Then I raised my eyes and looked south. It was there,
the Place of the Gods.

How can I tell what it was like—you do not know. It

145 was there, in the red light, and they were too big, to be
houses. It was there with the red light upon it, mighty and
*ruined. I knew that in another moment the gods would
see me. I *covered my eyes with my hands and crept
back into the forest.

150   Surely, that was enough to do, and live. Surely it was
enough to spend the night upon the cliff. The Forest
People themselves do not come near. Yet, all through the
night, I knew that I should have to cross the river and walk
in the places of the gods, although the gods *ate me up.

155 My magic did not help me at all and yet there was a fire in
my *bowels, a fire in my mind. When the sun rose, I
thought : " My journey has been clean. Now I will go
home from my journey." But, even as I thought so, I
knew I could not. If I went to the place of the gods, I

---

133. ə'pɑːt. — 137. biˈlou; dʒaiənt. — 139. ˈθəːsti; ˈouˈdis ˈsʌn;
ˈseikrɪd. — 147. ruɪnd. — 148. ˈkʌvəd. — 154. et. — 156. bauəlz.

THE " GOD-ROADS " OF AMERICA TO-DAY.

160 would *undoubtedly die, but, if I did not go, I could never
     be at peace with my spirit again. It is better to lose one's
     life than one's spirit, if one is a priest and the son of a priest.
         Nevertheless, as I made the *raft, the *tears ran out of my
     eyes. The Forest People could have killed me without
165 fight, if they had come upon me then, but they did not come.
     When the raft was made, I said the sayings for the dead
     and *painted myself for death. My heart was cold as a frog
     and my knees like water, but the burning in my mind would
     not let me have peace. As I *pushed the raft from the
170 shore, I began my death song—I had the right. It was a
     fine song.
         " I am John, son of John, " I sang. " My people are the
         Hill People. They are the men.
     I go into the Dead Places but I am not slain.
175 I take the metal from the Dead Places but I am not
         *blasted.
     I travel upon the god-roads and am not afraid.
         *E-yah !   I have killed the panther, I have killed the
         fawn !
180 E-yah ! I have come to the great river. No man has
         come there before.
     It is forbidden to go east, but I have gone, forbidden
         to go on the great river, but I am there.
     Open your hearts, you spirits, and hear my song.
185 Now I go to the place of the gods, I shall not return.
     My body is painted for death and my limbs weak, but
         my heart is big as I go to the place of the gods ! "
         All the same, when I came to the Place of the Gods, I
     was afraid, afraid. The *current of the great river is very
190 strong—it gripped my raft with its hands. That was magic,
     for the river itself is wide and calm. I could feel evil spirits
     about me, in the bright morning; I could feel their breath
     on my neck as I was swept down the stream. Never have I
     been so much alone—I tried to think of my knowledge, but

     160. ʌn'dautɪdlɪ. — 163. raːft; tɪez. 167. 'peɪntɪd. — 169. puʃt.
     — 176. 'blɑːstɪd. — 178. 'ɪː'jɑː. — 189. 'kʌrənt.

A VIEW OF " THE PLACE OF THE GODS "
ACROSS THE RIVER "OU-DIS-SUN ".

195 it was a squirrel's heap of winter nuts. There was no
strength in my knowledge any more and I felt small and
*naked as a new-hatched bird—alone upon the great river,
the servant of the gods.

Yet, after a while, my eyes were opened and I saw. I
200 saw both banks of the river—I saw that once there had
been god-roads across it, though now they were broken
and fallen like broken vines. Very great they were, and
wonderful and broken—broken in the time of the Great
Burning when the fire fell out of the sky. And always the
205 current took me nearer to the place of the Gods, and the
*huge ruins rose before my eyes.

I do not know the *customs of rivers—we are the People
of the Hills. I tried to *guide my raft with the pole, but it
spun around. I thought the river meant to take me past the
210 Place of the Gods and out into the Bitter Water of the
*legends. I *grew angry then—my heart felt strong. I
said aloud : " I am a priest and the son of a priest ! " The
gods heard me—they showed me how to paddle with the
pole on one side of the raft. The current changed itself—I
215 drew near to the Place of the Gods.

When I was very near, my raft struck and turned over.
I can swim in our lakes—I swam to the shore. There was
a great spike of rusted metal sticking out into the river—I
*hauled myself up upon it and sat there, *panting. I had
220 saved my bow and two arrows and the knife I found in the
Dead Place, but that was all. My raft went *whirling
*downstream toward the Bitter Water. I looked after it,
and thought if it had trod me under, at least I would be
safely dead. Nevertheless, when I had dried my bow-
225 string and *re-strung it, I walked forward to the Place of the
Gods.

It felt like ground underfoot; it did not burn me. It is
not true what some of the tales say, that the ground there
burns for ever, for I have been there. Here and there were

197. 'neikid. — 206. hju:dʒ. — 207. 'kʌstəmz. — 208. gaid. —
211. 'ledʒəndz; gru:. — 219. hɔːld; 'pæntiŋ. — 221. 'hwəːliŋ. —
222. 'daunstriːm. — 225. 'riːˈstrʌŋ.

the marks and stains of the Great Burning, on the ruins, that 230
is true. But they were old marks and old stains. It is not
true either, what some of our priests say, that it is an island
covered with fogs and *enchantments. It is not. It is a
great Dead Place—greater than any Dead Place we know.
Everywhere in it there are god-roads, though most are 235
cracked and broken. Everywhere there are the ruins of
the high *towers of the gods.

233. inˈtʃɑːntmənts. — 237. tauəz.

NOTES

3. Dead Places : the former towns of men. — **4.** metal : in the uncivilized state of the world described here, metal is very scarce, and has become the object of a cult. — **6.** purified : by some kind of religious ceremony or prayer. — **8.** the Place of the Gods : it will appear later that this was the name given to the ruins of New York. — **12.** the Great Burning : the author supposes that New York has been almost entirely destroyed in a great fire, probably in the course of a war. — **17.** my heart... weak : an attempt to express the physical impression accompanying lack of courage. — **18.** spirit : phantom. — **20.** fitting : proper. — **21.** kept my voice still : did not shout. — **26.** so he knew... : there is a good deal of superstition in the cult of metal. — **29.** good hunters : tha society lives mainly from hunting, tso a good hunter is an efficient member of the community; the good piece... fire : a future priest being a superior creature is already treated with respect. — **32.** boasted : expressed pride. — **39.** chants: religious songs; spells : magical incantations. — **40.** running : flowing. — **43.** it does not hurt them : it is becoming visible that the priests in this society keep all the knowledge to themselves, and impose upon the ignorance of the others (the hunters). — **48.** the gods : the men of the time before the Great Burning. — **53.** the Forest People : the writer is a priest of the Hill People, who consider themselves as far superior to the other tribes. — **54.** the (spinning-) wheel : *rouet*. — **55.** grubs : worms. — **60.** on my journey : a ritual journey, necessary for the young man to become a full priest; leave : permission. — **61.** stroking : caressing. — **63.** the house of the priesthood : the temple. — **64.** a cool stone : the coldest thing the young man can think of to express his self-control. — **71.** stern : severe. — **73.** waved : undulated. — **75.** outer chamber : of the temple, the inner chamber being reserved for the priests; buzzing : *bourdonnement*. — **80.** threw the sticks : a primitive process of fortune-telling. — **82.** eat you up : devour you, kill you. — **85.** sounded thin : had a very weak sound. — **98.** fasting : eating nothing, for purification. — **103.** still : motionless and silent. — **105.** deer : *cerfs*. — **106.** wind me : become aware of my presence through the sense of smelling. —

107. fawn : *faon*. — **111.** hummed : made a continuous murmuring sound; with : because of. — **117.** tearing at : trying to tear, with its paws. — **118.** meant : destined. — **120.** eight suns : eight days (a measure of distance as well as time for those primitive people). — **124.** rusted : (of iron) damaged by water; to : in comparison with. — **125.** feel big : swell (with pride or happiness). — **126.** game : *gibier*. — **129.** clean : not impure. — **132.** the god-road : the road made by the gods (that is, of course, by men). — **134.** safer going : less dangerous to travel through; a long way off : from a long distance. — **139.** Ou-dis-sun : the real name of this river, near and in New York, is Hudson. — **148.** crept back : went back surreptitiously. — **150.** that : seeing the Place of the Gods from a distance. — **152.** all through : during all. — **156.** bowels : entrails. — **163.** raft : flat wooden structure made to float on the water. — **166.** sayings : formulas. — **167.** painted myself : another primitive custom or rite of magic. — **168.** like water : very weak. — **173.** the men : the only men, superior to the Forest People. — **174.** slain : killed (to slay, I slew). — **176.** blasted : destroyed (as) by lightning. — **178.** E-yah : a kind of meaningless war-cry. — **190.** gripped : seized strongly. — **191.** evil : malevolent. — **193.** swept : was carried rapidly. — **195.** a squirrel's... nuts : something contemptible and inefficient. — **197.** new-hatched : having recently come out of its egg. — **199.** a while : a short time. — **201.** god-roads across it : bridges. — **204.** when the fire fell out of the sky : a superstitious expression, probably referring to air-bombing. — **208.** the pole : a long piece of wood. — **209.** spun around : turned rapidly round; past : beyond. — **210.** the Bitter Water : the ocean, probably representing in that religion hell. — **213.** to paddle : *pagayer*. — **215.** drew near to : approached. — **216.** struck (a rock). — **218.** spike : point; sticking out : appearing above the surface. — **219.** hauled myself up : *me hissai;* panting : breathing rapidly. — **221.** whirling : turning rapidly round and round. — **223.** trod me under : crushed under itself (to tread, I trod). — **225.** re-strung : placed the string back in its proper position. — **227.** felt like : gave the same impression as. — **231.** stains : dark traces. — **237.** the high towers : the sky-scrapers.

THÈME D'IMITATION

L'accident.

Après que j'eus quitté la maison de mes amis, qui me montrèrent comment regagner la ville, je pris la route principale pour aller vers le Sud. Il est défendu de rouler à gauche sur cette route, même pour dépasser une autre voiture ou pour tourner. A un carrefour où j'avais le droit de passer le premier, selon la loi, une automobile heurta la mienne. Je fus d'abord très effrayé, car jamais auparavant je n'avais eu d'accident. Mais il ne conve-

'nait pas qu'un conducteur expérimenté se montrât craintif. Dès que je n'eus plus peur, mes yeux s'ouvrirent et j'essayai de me lever; malheureusement il n'y avait plus de force dans mes jambes, et je dus rester assis, attendant ce qui allait arriver. Comment dire à quoi ressemblait la voiture de l'autre conduc-teur? Je ne sais comment la décrire. Tout de même, c'est lui qui avait commis une erreur, et quand un gendarme parut, je demandai et obtins des dommages et intérêts.

VERSION AVEC QUESTIONS

The Noble Savage.

To come to the point at once, I beg to say that I have not the least belief in the Noble Savage. I consider him a prodigious nuisance, and an enormous superstition. His calling rum fire-water, and me a pale face, wholly fails to reconcile me to him. I don't care what he calls me. I call him a savage, and I call a savage something highly desirable to be civilized off the face of the earth. I think a mere gent (which I take to be the lowest form of civilization) better than a howling, whistling, clucking, stamping, jumping, tearing savage. It is all one to me, whether he sticks a fish-bone through his visage, or bits of trees through the lobes of his ears, or birds' feathers in his hair; whether he flattens his head between two boards, or spreads his nose over the breadth of his face, or drags his lower lip down by great weights, or blackens his teeth, or knocks them out, or paints one cheek red and the other blue, or tattooes himself, or oils himself, or rubs his body with fat, or crimps it with knives. Yielding to whichsoever of these agreeable eccentricities, he is a savage — cruel, false, thievish, murderous; a wild animal with the questionable gift of boasting; a conceited, tiresome, blood-thirsty, monotonous humbug.

Charles DICKENS, *Reprinted Pieces.*

QUESTIONS : 1. *Express in another way the idea contained in* civilized off the face of the earth, *and write two or three sentences with similar constructions.* — 2. *What points in Dicken's criticism of the savage appear to you to be exaggerated ?* — 3. *What aspects of the society described in Benét's story would Dickens have disap-proved of ?*

QUESTIONNAIRE

Where can all men go ? — What is the property of metal ? — What is the real name of the Place of the Gods ? — How was the modern world destroyed ? — What did the narrator do while his father visited a dead house ? — How did the priest know that his son would be a priest ? — How was the future priest treated at home ? — What kind of things did priests know ? — What makes the superiority of the Hill People over the Forest People ? — How was the young priest purified before his journey ? — What did he often dream of ? — What weapons did his father give him ? — How did the young priest choose the direction of his journey ? — Relate the killing of the panther. — How did he interpret his luck in finding a knife ? — How far was the great river ? — What is a god-road ? — What prevented the young man from going home after he had seen the river ? — How did he cross the river ? — What useful preparation did he make for death ? — What did the death-song consist of ? — What were the young man's feelings and thoughts while on the river ? — What was the aspect of the bridges across the river ? — Was the young priest a skilful boatman ? — Who helped him in his difficulties ? — How did he escape from death on the river ? — Did the ground burn him ? — What did he think of the great city ?

INTONATION

(Émotionnelle, descendante, affirmation emphatique.)

82. This is a \very strong dream, he said ‖

(Neutre, ascendante, sous-entendu ironique.)

121. The ⁻Forest −People are a‿fraid of them ↑

(Émotionnelle, descendante, affirmation emphatique.)

170. It was a \fine song. ‖

(Neutre, descendante, affirmation simple.)

236. ⁻Everywhere there are the ⁻ruins of the− high ⁻towers of
                                      the \gods ‖

II. THE GREAT SECRET OF
THE TOWERS OF THE GODS

How shall I tell what I saw? I went carefully, my strung
bow in my hand, my skin ready for *danger. There should
have been the *wailings of spirits and the *shrieks of
*demons, but there were not. It was very silent and sunny
where I had landed—the wind and the rain and the birds 5
that drop seeds had done their work—the grass grew in
the cracks of the broken stone. It is a fair *island—no
wonder the gods built there. If I had come there, a god, I
also would have built.

How shall I tell what I saw? The towers are not all 10
broken—here and there one still stands, like a great tree
in a forest, and the birds nest high. But the towers themselves look blind, for the gods are gone. I saw a *fish-
hawk, catching fish in the river. I saw a little *dance of
white *butterflies over a great heap of broken stones and 15
*columns. I went there and looked about me—there
was a carved stone with cut-letters, broken in half. I can
read letters but I could not understand these. They said
*UBTREAS. There was also the *shattered image of a man
or a god. It had been made of white stone and he wore his 20
hair tied back like a woman's. His name was *ASHING, as
I read on the cracked half of a stone. I thought it wise to
pray to ASHING, though I do not know that god.

How shall I tell what I saw? There was no smell of
man left, on stone or metal. Nor were there many trees in 25
that *wilderness of stone. There are many pigeons, nest-

2. 'deinʒə. — 3. 'weilɪŋz; ʃrɪːks. — 4. 'diːmənz. — 7. 'ailənd. —
13. 'fiʃhɔːk. — 14. dɑːns. — 15. 'bʌtəflaiz. — 16. 'kɔləmz. —
19. 'ʌhtrɪəs; 'ʃætəd. — 21. 'æʃɪŋ. — 26. 'wildənis.

ing and dropping in the towers—the gods must have loved them, or, perhaps, they used them for *sacrifices.   There are wild cats that roam the god-roads, green-eyed, *unafraid
30 of man.   At night they wail like demons, but they are not demons.   The wild dogs are more *dangerous, for they hunt in a pack, but them I did not meet till later.   Everywhere there are the carved stones, carved with *magical numbers or words.

35   I went North—I did not try to hide myself.   When a god or a demon saw me, then I would die, but meanwhile I was no longer afraid.   My hunger for knowledge burned in me—there was so much that I could not understand.   After awhile, I knew that my belly was hungry.   I could have
40 hunted for my meat, but I did not hunt.   It is known that the gods did not hunt as we do—they got their food from *enchanted boxes and jars.   Sometimes these are still found in the Dead Places—once, when I was a child and foolish, I opened such a jar and *tasted it and found the food sweet.
45 But my father found out and punished me for it strictly, for, often, that food is death.   Now, though, I had long gone past what was forbidden, and I entered the *likeliest towers, looking for the food of the gods.

      I found it at last in the ruins of a great temple in the mid-
50 city.   A mighty temple it must have been, for the roof was painted like the sky at night with its stars—that much I could see, though the *colours were faint and dim.   It went down into great caves and *tunnels—perhaps they kept their slaves there.   But when I started to *climb down, I
55 heard the *squeaking of rats, so I did not go—rats are unclean, and there must have been many tribes of them, from the squeaking.   But near there, I found food, in the heart of a ruin, behind a door that still opened.   I ate only the fruits from the jars—they had a very sweet taste.   There
60 was drink, too, in bottles of glass—the drink of the gods was

---

28. 'sækrifaɪsɪz. — 29. ˈʌnəˈfreid. —31. deɪnʒərəs. — 33. ˈmædʒɪkəl.
— 42. ɪnˈtʃɑːntɪd. — 44. teɪstɪd. — 47. ˈlaɪklɪst. — 52. ˈkʌləz. —
53. ˈtʌnəlz. — 54. ˈklaɪm. — 55. ˈskwiːkɪŋ).

THE TOWERS OF THE GODS.

strong and made my head swim. After I had eaten and
drunk, I slept on the top of a stone, my bow at my side.

When I woke, the sun was low. Looking down from
where I lay, I saw a dog sitting on his *haunches. His
65 tongue was hanging out of his mouth; he looked as if he were
laughing. He was a big dog, with a grey-brown coat, as big
as a *wolf. I sprang up and shouted at him but he did not
move—he just sat there as if he were laughing. I did not
like that. When I reached for a stone to throw, he moved
70 swiftly out of the way of the stone. He was not afraid of
me; he looked at me as if I were meat. No doubt I could
have killed him with an arrow, but I did not know if there
were others. *Moreover, night was falling.

I looked about me—not far away there was a great,
75 broken god-road, leading North. The towers were high
enough, but not so high and while many of the dead-
houses were *wrecked, there were some that stood. I went
toward this god-road, keeping to the *heights of the ruins,
while the dog followed. When I had reached the god-road,
80 I saw that there were others behind him. If I had slept
later, they would have come upon me *asleep and torn out
my throat. As it was, they were sure enough of me; they
did not *hurry. When I went into the dead-house, they
kept watch at the *entrance—doubtless they thought they
85 would have a fine hunt. But a dog cannot open a door and
I knew, from the books, that the gods did not like to live on
the ground but on high.

I had just found a door I could open when the dogs
decided to rush. Ha ! They were surprised when I shut
90 the door in their faces—it was a good door, of strong metal.
I could hear their foolish *baying beyond it, but I did not
stop to answer them. I was in darkness—I found stairs and
climbed. There were many stairs, turning around till my
head was *dizzy. At the top was another door—I found the
95 *knob and opened it. I was in a long small *chamber—on

64. 'hɔːntʃɪz. — 67. wulf. — 73. mɔə'rouvə. — 77. rekt. —
78. haits. — 81. ə'slɪːp. — 83. 'hʌrɪ. — 84. 'entrəns. — 91. 'beiiŋ.
— 94. 'dizi. — 95. nɔb; 'tʃeimbə.

one side of it was a *bronze door that could not be opened,
for it had no handle. Perhaps there was a magic word to
open it, but I did not have the word. I turned to the door
in the *opposite side of the wall. The lock of it was
broken and I opened it and went in.   100

Within, there was a place of great *riches. The god
who lived there must have been a powerful god. The first
room was a small *ante-room—I waited there for some time,
telling the spirits of the place that I came in peace and not
as a robber. When it seemed to me that they had had time 105
to hear me, I went on. Ah, what riches ! Few, even, of
the windows had been broken—it was all as it had been.
The great windows that looked over the city had not been
broken at all, though they were dusty and *streaked with
many years. There were coverings on the floors, the   110
colours not greatly faded, and chairs were soft and deep.
There were *pictures upon the walls, very strange, very
wonderful—I remember one of a bunch of flowers in a jar
—if you came close to it, you could see nothing but bits
of colour, but if you stood away from it, the flowers might 115
have been picked yesterday. It made my heart feel strange
to look at this picture—and to look at the figure of a bird, in
some hard clay, on a table and see it so like our birds.
Everywhere there were books and writings, many in
*tongues that I could not read. The god who lived there 120
must have been a wise god and full of knowledge. I felt
I had right there, as I *sought knowledge also.

Nevertheless, it was strange. There was a washing-
place but no water—perhaps the gods washed in air. There
was a cooking-place but no wood, and though there was a 125
*machine to cook food, there was no place to put fire in it.
Nor were there candles or lamps—there were things that
looked like lamps, but they had neither oil nor wick. All
these things were magic, but I touched them and lived—
the magic had gone out of them. Let me tell one thing to 130

96. brɔnz. — 99. 'ɔpəzit. — 101. 'ritʃiz. — 103. 'æntirum. —
109. striːkt. — 112. 'piktʃəz. — 120. tʌŋz. — 122. sɔːt. — 126. mə-
'ʃiːn.

show. In the washing-place, a thing said " Hot. " but it was not hot to the touch—another thing said " Cold ", but it was not cold. This must have been a strong magic, but the magic was gone. I do not understand—they had
135 ways—I wish that I knew.

It was close and dry and dusty in their house of the gods. I have said the magic was gone, but that is not true—it had gone from the magic things, but it had not gone from the place. I felt the spirits about me, *weighing upon me.
140 Nor had I ever slept in a Dead Place before—and yet, tonight I must sleep there. When I thought of it, my tongue felt dry in my throat, in spite of my wish for knowledge. Almost I would have gone down again and faced the dogs, but I did not.

145 I had not gone through all the rooms when the darkness fell. When it fell, I went back to the big room looking over the city and made fire. There was a place to make fire and a box with wood in it, though I do not think they cooked there. I *wrapped myself in a floor-covering and slept in
150 front of the fire—I was very tired.

Now I tell what is very strong magic. I woke in the midst of the night. When I woke, the fire had gone out and I was cold. It seemed to me that all around me there were *whisperings and voices. I closed my eyes to shut
155 them out. Some will say that I slept again, but I do not think that I slept. I could feel the spirits drawing my spirit out of my body as a fish is drawn on a line.

Why should I lie about it? I am a priest and the son of a priest. If there are spirits, as they say, in the small Dead
160 Places near us, what spirits must there not be in that great Place of the Gods? And would not they wish to speak? After such long years? I know that I felt myself drawn as a fish is drawn on a line. I had stepped out of my body—I could see my body asleep in front of the cold fire, but it
165 was not I. I was drawn to look out upon the city of the gods.

139. 'weiiŋ. — 149. ræpt. — 154. 'wispəriŋz.

LIGHTS, LINES OF LIGHTS....

BY THE WATERS OF BABYLON

It should have been dark, for it was night, but it was not
dark. Everywhere there were lights—lines of light—
*circles and *blurs of light—ten thousand *torches would
not have been the same. The sky itself was *alight —you
170 could barely see the stars for the glow in the sky. I thought
to myself : " This is strong magic, " and trembled. There
was a *roaring in my ears like the rushing of rivers. Then
my eyes grew used to the light and my ears to the sound. I
knew that I was seeing the city as it had been when the gods
175 were alive.

That was a sight indeed—yes, that was a sight : I could
not have seen it in the body—my body would have died.
Everywhere went the gods, on foot and in *chariots—there
were gods beyond number and counting and their chariots
180 blocked the streets. They had turned night to day for their
*pleasure—they did not sleep with the sun. The noise of
their coming and going was the noise of many waters. It
was magic what they could do—it was magic what they did.

I looked out of another window—the great vines of their
185 bridges were *mended and the god-roads went East and
West. Restless, restless, were the gods and always in
*motion ! They *burrowed tunnels under rivers—they
flew in the air. With *unbelievable tools they did *giant
works—no part of the earth was safe from them, for, if they
190 wished for a thing, they *summoned it from the other side
of the world. And always, as they *laboured and rested, as
they feasted and made love, there was a drum in their
ears—the pulse of the giant city, beating and beating like
a man's heart.

195 Were they happy? What is happiness to the gods?
They were great, they were mighty, they were wonderful
and terrible. As I looked upon them and their magic, I
felt like a child—but a little more, it seemed to me, and
they would lay their hands upon the stars. I saw them

168. 'səːklz; bləːz; 'tɔːtʃiz. — 169. ə'lait. — 172. 'rɔːrin. — 178.
'tʃæriəts. — 181. 'pleʒə. — 185. 'mendid. — 187. 'mouʃən; 'bʌroud.
— 188. ˌʌnbi'liːvəbl; dʒaiənt. — 190. 'sʌmənd. — 191. 'leibəd.

with *wisdom beyond wisdom and knowledge beyond 200
knowledge. And yet not all they did was well done—even
I could see that—and yet their wisdom could not but grow
until all was peace.

Then I saw their fate come upon them and that was
terrible past speech. It came upon them as they walked 205
the streets of their city. I have been in the fights with the
Forest People—I have seen men die. But this was not like
that. When gods war with gods, they use weapons we do
not know. It was fire falling out of the sky and a mist that
*poisoned. It was the time of the Great Burning and the 210
*Destruction. They ran about like *ants in the streets of
their city—poor gods, poor gods ! Then the towers began
to fall. A few *escaped—yes, a few. The legends tell it.
But, even after the city had become a Dead Place, for many
years the poison was still in the ground. I saw it happen, 215
I saw the last of them die. It was darkness over the broken
city and I wept.

All this, I saw. I saw it as I have told it, though not in
the body. When I woke in the morning, I was hungry, but
I did not think first of my hunger, for my heart was *per- 220
plexed and *confused. I knew the reason for the Dead
Places, but I did not see why it had happened. It seemed
to me it should not have happened, with all the magic they
had. I went through the house looking for an answer.
There was so much in the house I could not understand— 225
and yet I am a priest and the son of a priest. It was like
being on the side of the great river, at night, with no light
to show the way.

Then I saw the dead god. He was sitting in his chair, by
the window, in a room I had not entered before and, for 230
the first moment, I thought that he was alive. Then I saw
the skin on the back of his hand—it was like dry *leather.
The room was shut, hot and dry—no doubt that had kept
him as he was. At first I was afraid to *approach him

200. 'wizdəm. — 210. 'pɔizənd. — 211. di'strʌkʃen; ænts. —
213. i'skeipt. — 220. pə'plekst. — 221. kən'fjuːzd. — 232. 'leðə. —
234. ə'proutʃ.

235　—then the fear left me. He was sitting looking out over
　　　his city—he was dressed in the clothes of the gods. His
　　　age was neither young or old—I could not tell his age.
　　　But there was wisdom in his face and great sadness. You
　　　could see that he would have not run away. He had sat at
240　his window, watching his city die—then he himself had
　　　died. But it is better to *lose one's life than one's spirit—
　　　and you could see from the face that his spirit had not
　　　been *lost. I knew, that, if I touched him, he would fall
　　　into dust—and yet, there was something *unconquered
245　in the face.
　　　　　That is all of my story, for then I knew he was a man—
　　　I knew then that they had been men, neither gods nor
　　　demons. It is a great knowledge, hard to tell and *believe.
　　　They were men—they went a dark road, but they were
250　men. I had no fear after that—I had no fear going home,
　　　though twice I fought off the dogs and once I was hunted
　　　for two days by the Forest People. When I saw my father
　　　again, I prayed and was purified. He touched my lips and
　　　my breast; he said : " You went away a boy. You come
255　back a man and a priest." I said : " Father, they were
　　　men ! I have been in the Place of the Gods and seen it !
　　　Now slay me, if it is the law—but still I know they were
　　　men. "
　　　　　He looked at me out of both eyes. He said : " The law is
260　not always the same shape—you have done what you have
　　　done. I could not have done it my time, but you come
　　　after me. Tell ! "
　　　　　I told and he listened. After that, I wished to tell all the
　　　people but he showed me *otherwise. He said : " Truth is
265　a hard deer to hunt. If you eat too much truth at once,
　　　you may die of the truth. It was not idly that our fathers
　　　*forbade the Dead Places. " He was right—it is better
　　　the truth should come little by little. I have learned that,
　　　being a priest. Perhaps, in the old days, they ate know-
270　ledge too fast.

　　　　　241. luːz. — 243. lɔst. — 244. ʌnˈkɔŋkəd. — 248. biˈliːv. —
　　　264. ˈʌðəwaiz. — 267. fəˈbæd.

Nevertheless, we make a beginning. It is not for the metal alone we go to the Dead Places now—there are the books and the writings. They are hard to learn. And the magic tools are broken—but we can look at them and wonder. At least, we make a beginning. And, when I am chief priest, we shall go beyond the great river. We shall go to the Place of the Gods—the place newyork—not one man but a *company. We shall look for the images of the gods and find the god ASHING and the others—the gods *Lincoln and *Biltmore and *Moses. But they were men who built the city, not gods or demons. They were men. I remember the dead man's face. They were men who were here before us. We must build again.

275

280

278. 'kʌmpənı. — 280. 'lınkən; 'bıltmɔə; 'mouziz.

NOTES

1. my strung bow : my bow with the string ready for shooting. — **3.** wailings : lamentations; shrieks : shrill cries. — **7.** no wonder : it is not surprising that. — **12.** nest : make their nests. — **13.** fish-hawk : *aigle pêcheur.* — **17.** carved : sculptured; cut-letters : engraved letters. — **19.** Ubtreas : letters from the name of the building (subtreasury); shattered : broken violently into pieces. — **21.** tied back : kept back by a string or ribbon, according to the fashion of the 18th century; Ashing : obviously part of the name of George Washington (1732-1799). — **22.** wise : prudent (in case he should be a powerful god). — **26.** wilderness : desert. — **27.** dropping : flying swiftly downwards, as if they were falling. — **29.** roam : wander about on. — **32.** in a pack : *en meute.* — **39.** belly : a word (not used in polite conversation) for stomach. — **42.** jars : pots. — **44.** sweet : having a pleasant taste, similar to that of sugar. —

45. found out : discovered what I had done. — **46.** I had long gone past : I had already done many things worse than. — **47.** likeliest : most promising. — **49.** in the mid-city : in the middle of the city. — **51.** that much : (vulgar for) so much. — **52.** faint : not bright; dim : not clear; it : the temple. — **53.** caves : caverns. — **55.** squeaking : cry. — **56.** tribes : *tribus.* — **61.** made my head swim : made me unsteady and dizzy. — **64.** haunches : the posterior part of the body. — **66.** coat : *pelage.* — **69.** reached for : moved my arm towards. — **77.** wrecked : devastated. — **78.** keeping to the heights : remaining on the summits. — **81.** torn out (to tear, I tore) : lacerated. — **82.** as it was : in the present circumstances, things being what they were; of (getting) me. — **84.** to keep watch : *monter la garde.* — **87.** on high : at a high level. — **91.** baying : the cry of dogs. — **94.** dizzy : as if he had been again drinking " the drink of the gods ".

— **95.** knob : (of a door) *bouton.* — **105.** robber : thief. — **109.** streaked : covered with streaks or parallel lines (of dirt). — **110.** coverings on the floors : (carpets). — **111.** faded : of diminished brightness. — **113.** bunch : bouquet. — **114.** bits : small fragments (obviously, this picture belonged to the *pointilliste* school of painting). — **115.** (looked as if they) might have been picked. — **118.** clay : *argile.* — **120.** tongues : languages. — **122.** I had right (to be) there; sought : was trying to find (to seek, I sought, sought). — **128.** wick : *mèche.* — **129.** lived : did not die at once (from the magic). — **131.** a thing said " Hot " : the word " Hot " was written on a thing (a water-tap). — **135.** ways : particular methods. — **136.** close : *renfermé.* — **139.** weighing upon me : making me feel the heavy weight of their presence. — **149.** wrapped : enveloped. — **154.** whisperings : murmurs; to shut them out : to exclude them. — **158.** lie : tell something false. — **163.** stepped : walked, moved. — **168.** blurs : big spots. — **169.** alight : illuminated. — **170.** barely : hardly; for : because of; the glow : reddish light. — **172.** roaring : loud noise (like lion's voice); rushing : swift motion. — **177.** in the body :

if I had been in my body, in my normal condition. — **179.** beyond number and counting : innumerable. — **180.** turned : changed. — **181.** with : at the same time as. — **184.** the great vines of : (the former metaphor is continued here). — **187.** burrowed : dug, like rabbits. — **189.** safe from : inaccessible to. — **190.** summoned it : ordered it to come. — **192.** feasted : ate banquets ; made love : courted women. — **198.** but a little more : if they had had only a little more time or power. — **200.** beyond : surpassing the utmost extent of. — **202.** could not but : must unavoidably. — **204.** fate : destiny. — **205.** past speech : unspeakably. — **208.** war : fight in war. — **209.** It was fire... poisoned : incendiary bombs and poison gas. — **244.** unconquered : not defeated. — **251.** fought off : turned away by fighting. — **257.** slay : kill. — **264.** he showed me otherwise : he gave me reasons for acting differently. — **266.** not idly : not without good reason. — **278.** a company : a large number of people. — **281.** Lincoln : (Abraham), 1809-1865, one of the greatest American statesmen; Biltmore : the name of a big hotel in New York; Moses : the name of the New York " Parks and Roads Commissioner ".

THÈME D'IMITATION

La visite du vieux port.

En arrivant dans le vieux port, Jean regarda autour de lui. Il avait depuis longtemps dépassé la dernière rangée de maisons, et il aurait pu continuer à suivre la digue sans se tromper de direction. Mais, puisqu'il cherchait à se renseigner sur le passé du port, il jugea prudent de s'adresser à un marin. Ce dernier, qui, la pipe à la bouche, avait l'air de s'ennuyer, lui montra le plus célèbre des anciens bassins, où aucun bateau n'était entré depuis dix ans, surmonté d'un phare dont la lumière s'était éteinte; et il n'y avait guère d'eau dans ce bassin; on n'y voyait que des algues et des galets. Il aurait dû y avoir une pancarte pour indiquer aux visiteurs l'histoire de ce vieux port; mais Jean, qui ne venait pas en flâneur ordinaire, écouta avec passion le récit du marin. Il venait de le quitter quand il s'aperçut que le soleil se couchait. Le dernier train avait dû quitter la gare, et il allait lui falloir dormir dans la petite ville pittoresque mais inconfortable.

VERSION AVEC QUESTIONS

The Progress of City-lighting.

God bless the lamplighter, indeed   For the term of his twilight diligence is near at hand; and for not much longer shall we watch him speeding up the street, and, at measured intervals, knocking another luminous hole into the dusk. The Greeks would have made a noble myth of such an one; how he distributed starlight, and, as soon as the need was over, re-collected it; and the little lantern, which was his instrument, and held enough fire to kindle a whole parish, would have been fitly commemorated in the legend. Now, like all heroic tasks, his labours draw towards apotheosis, and in the light of victory himself shall disappear. For another advance has been effected. Our tame stars are to come out in future, not one by one, but all in a body and at once. A sedate electrician somewhere in a back office touches a spring — and behold! from one end to another of the city, from east to west, there is light ! *Fiat Lux*, says the sedate electrician. What a spectacle, on some clear, dark nightfall, from the edge of Hampstead Hill, when in a moment, in the twinkling of an eye, the design of the monstrous city flashes into vision — a glittering hieroglyph many square miles in extent; and when, to borrow and debase an image, all the evening street lamps burst into song! Such is the spectacle of the future, preluded the other day by an experiment in Pall Mall. Star-rise by electricity, the most romantic flight of civilization; the compensatory benefit for an innumerable array of factories and bankers' clerks.

Robert Louis STEVENSON, *A Plea for Gas Lamps.*

QUESTIONS : 1. *Do you think the writer prefers gas-lamps or electricity ? Give your reasons.* — 2. *Can you imagine a Greek-like myth for the electrician as well as for the lamp-lighter ?* — 4. *Do you regret the disappearance of gas-lamps ?.* — 4. *Why is it necessary to compensate for factories and bankers' clerks ?*

QUESTIONNAIRE

What should there have been in the City of the Gods ? — What had been the effect of wind and rain and birds there ? — Were all the towers broken ? — What letters did the young priest read on monuments ? — Why did he fail to understand them ? — Why are wild dogs more dangerous than wild cats ? — What kind of food did the young man look for ? — In what circumstances had he already tasted tinned food ? — What prevented him from going down into the building he had entered ? — Did he like the drink of the gods ? — What feelings did the dog's expression remind him of when he woke ? — How did he escape from the dogs ? — What was his impression when he saw the pictures ? — What surprised him in the bath-room and the kitchen ? — What kind of details did he consider as magic ? — Had the magic completely left the house ? — Where did the young priest sleep ? — What happened when he woke in the middle of the night ? — Do you think he went to sleep again ? — Did he think so ? — What did he see when he looked out of the window ? — How was the city destroyed ? — Do you think there is anything unlikely in the author's hypothesis about the future of America, as described here ? — What made the young priest finally understand who were the gods of New York ? — Did he like and admire the dead "god" that he found ? — How did the young man's father receive him on his return ? — Why did they not tell the whole truth to everybody ? — When did the young man intend to return to "newyork" ? — What kind of men did he consider as gods ? — What beginning did he at once make ? — How did the young man come to his resolution for the future ? — Do you think it wise ?

INTONATION

(Neutre, descendante, question commençant par mot interrogatif.)
1. ⁻How shall I ⁻tell what I ＼saw ‖

(Neutre, ascendante, sous-entendu.)
68. I did ⁻not ₋like ／that ↑ '

(Émotionnelle, descendante, affirmation emphatique.)
171. This is ＼strong magic ‖

(Neutre, ascendante, phrase inachevée.)
219. When I ⁻woke in the ₋morning ↑

www.ingramcontent.com/pod-product-compliance
Lightning Source LLC
Chambersburg PA
CBHW031241260626
47169CB00007B/2401